MW00413618

What have I done?

Standing on the narrow country road, Iris watched the little bus slowly pull away.

A shiver, that had nothing to do with the chilly December night, started at the back of her neck and traveled all the way down her spine. She wished she had answered differently when the driver had asked, "Sure this is the right stop, miss?"

Now, the cheerful holiday music slowly faded away, and the tail lights shrank to tiny ruby dots in the twilight before the bus finally disappeared around a bend in the road.

What have I done?

This is a work of fiction. Except for historical figures and events, the names, characters, businesses, events, and incidents are the products of the author's imagination. Any resemblance to actual persons, living or dead, or actual events is purely coincidental.

The Family Tree

First Edition, December 6, 2016

Copyright © 2016 Cynthia Rinear Bethune
Updated March 2018

ISBN-13: 978-1543160604

The Family Tree

Cynthia Rinear Bethune

Dedicated with love

to

Kendall, Devon & Iris

Chapter One

"NOT OPEN THIS CHRISTMAS?"

Adele Gibson's startled question echoed the words resonating in her husband's mind at the doctor's suggestion.

"I strongly recommend you don't," Dr. Alford said, glancing at Adele and then back to Charles.

Why the devil can't they keep the place warmer? Charles thought, stepping down carefully from the examination table, suddenly feeling the air-conditioned chill of the stark and sterile room.

"We own a Christmas tree farm, Doc," Charles said, pulling on his flannel shirt, "It's our livelihood. We canna miss an entire season."

"That's right, we—"

The doctor held up his hand. "Believe me, Adele, I know what I'm suggesting. But better your livelihood for *one* season than risking your life, Charles."

When the doctor turned back to the medical chart on the counter and made his notes, Charles met his wife's eyes, her expression still mirroring his own feelings. Already trying to think of a way to honor the doctor's prescription for rest but open for business through the holidays, he was interrupted by the doctor as he swiveled around to face them again.

"Even if Alexander were home; even if you have a manager, Charles, you know it would still demand what little energy you have. That spring virus damaged your heart. You must allow yourself the chance to recover before taking on too much."

The late afternoon heat did not warm him, nor did Charles notice the golden California sunlight glinting from Placerville's main street storefront windows. Even the bribe of rocky road fudge from the Candy Strike Emporium that Adele had used to lure him back to the damn doctor in the first place no longer had any appeal. He shook his head as Adele nodded towards the shop, and she continued driving slowly through town.

Kids kicked soccer balls and played on the public playground, enjoying their last bit of summer freedom before school started the following week.

But, crisp, cold winter mornings were on Charles's mind; the whisper of the bow saw through the fragrant trunk of a balsam fir, the squeals of delight from the children as they watched their tree moving through the baler and being tied onto the family car.

Six months before, he would have laughed at the

doctor's caution about risking his life as hyperbole, but since the flu had laid him low for an entire month in the spring, it sometimes felt like it was all he could do just to get out of bed in the morning, much less run a Christmas tree farm through its busy season. But it was not just their livelihood, it was their *life*, he thought, holding back a sigh. He had been doing that enough lately, sighing, and knew it worried Adele. As she said, he was not the sort of man to sigh.

Behind the wheel, he knew Adele felt as chill and remote, but she braked, waved and smiled at their friends and neighbors on their way out of town.

He knew why she chose this long route home. Down the back road that led past Dawson's farm, the air was redolent with the sweet tang of freshly harvested alfalfa, the aroma enhanced by a settling humidity and the old cow barn.

Invariably, at this point in their journey, she would tell him how it reminded her of her father, and he would laugh and tell her how flattered the old man would be. But not today.

"We *could* call Alex—"

"We will *not* call Alexander," he answered, more brusquely than he intended. Not as brusquely as he felt, but was sorry for it when he saw tears start in her eyes.

"Our son would *want* to know, Charles. He would want to come back and help."

"He's made his decision and I'll not be dr-ragging him back for obligation or guilt."

He tried to soften his voice, but what he managed in tone, he gave away with the brogue that still crept back into his words from time to time after forty years of being transplanted from the Scottish Highlands to Northern California. He knew she considered the rolling r's and the Gaelic creeping back into his speech her early warning system.

And he knew she was upset herself or she would never have suggested it. After those forty years of marriage, he often thought she knew him better than he knew himself.

"Well then," she said, taking a firm grip on the wheel and squaring her shoulders, "we'll get by and do what we must, just as we have in the past!"

She sounded determined, and he had met few people with her kind of pragmatic optimism. Still, he knew that tonight, after her evening prayers when she thought he was asleep, she would cry for yet another loss.

Adele was not the sort of woman to cry, but they had experienced too many losses over the years.

Their second child, little Aurora Jean, was born with a heart defect and had lived less than a month. When their older son Andrew had gone away to university, he hadn't been sure if he wanted to dedicate his life to the Christmas tree farm. In his last year, after his sudden marriage and while awaiting the birth of his child, he wrote to say he wanted to bring his wife and child back to Placerville and to work with his family once again.

Only months later he was dead, hit by a drunk driver on his way home from work late one night. Taken so young and so senselessly, even before the birth of his daughter.

Another loss, Charles thought of little Iris, who disappeared with her devastated young mother soon afterwards. Andrew's widow never responded to their offers of help and hospitality. Charles had even traveled to Los Angeles to look for her, unbeknownst to Adele, but Jennifer had left school and moved from her last address. They could only keep them in their prayers and hope Jennifer would contact them one day.

They had counted on Alexander to remain near, to eventually take over the farm and he had never given them cause to think he wanted otherwise. In his second year at an agricultural college in Pennsylvania, he met a young lady whose father owned the largest tree farm in the state and then Alex, too, was lost, to distance and a pretty face.

Not opening for the Christmas season meant not only the loss of income but the satisfaction brought by the successful completion of their year. And, not meaning to take away any honor from the Lord Jesus Himself, Charles thought, running a Christmas tree farm was *his* reason for the season.

Charles stood in the living room, now bright with early evening sunlight pouring in from the large western windows, and quiet except for the sounds of Adele

fussing in the kitchen. Barley soup for dinner, he knew
from peeking in the crock pot earlier. He was grateful
he still had a good appetite despite the bone-deep
weariness that overpowered him several times a day.

Never so much as now, he thought, leaning on
the windowsill and still trying to absorb the doctor's
orders, looking out at the long rows of Scots pine and
balsam fir.

Being made to disregard his extensive list of
chores should be a relief, he thought, but it was not.
They could manage financially, he knew, and worried
more about the impact on the rhythm of the growing
and harvesting he had nurtured over the years.

He sighed and turned away from the window.

Now what? Charles thought, looking about the
farmhouse he had always loved as though he had never
seen it before. The kitchen and dining area, and the
living room were one big, open area with two alcoves
at one end of the living room. In one, Adele's Christmas
collections; teacups and saucers, teapots, and painted
tins with holiday scenes, some she collected herself, but
most were gifts from family and friends. Along one
wall were Adele's hand-painted ornaments, one for
each year they had been in business. Shelves full to
overflowing with Adele's books filled the other alcove.

Since his illness in the spring, he had taken to
browsing through her library, an eclectic mix of classics
and romance, histories and mysteries, and even a few
espionage thrillers and biographies of admirable
people. Many of the titles he had seen on the shelves

for decades. He glanced at the most recent one he had read, and smiled, remembering how Adele spoke of the characters as though they were old friends of hers that he had just been introduced to, and asked after them as though something new might have happened since she had last finished the book herself.

The living room was paneled with wide, horizontal pinewood planks. Varnished over a half century ago, the rich patina gleamed like a candlelit glass of finely-aged Glenturret whisky, and sheer white curtains luffed at the open window with each gust of the warm afternoon breeze.

Adele's cup and saucer sat on a nearby table, the white rose pattern today, he noticed, her reading glasses draped over the spine of a big, hardcover book opened on the arm of the chair. New friends, he thought, glancing warily at the outlandish title. Soft classical music played on the radio and the old green sofa was sometimes too comfortable to be resisted, especially lately.

He sighed.

The new ornament Adele was painting was an elegantly decorated Christmas tree with candles that seemed to glow with their own light from the small glass ball. Many customers said they came for the ornament as much as they did for a tree. Each year a new design, from winter landscapes on frosty blue to nativity scenes framed with evergreen garlands. Her mood of the moment sometime in August or September often decided the theme of the year. But...

Now what, he thought again, and once again glanced around the living room remembering when he walked in and met his father-in-law for the first time. The two men took to each other immediately, kindred spirits in their love for Adele and their interest in trees, even through the difficult decision to break the century-old family tradition and switch from apples to evergreens.

He had once hoped to hand down the business to one or both of his sons.

Glancing down at the array of family photographs in front of him, his gaze fell on Adele's favorite of Andrew and Alexander. Their mock duel; fencing with long boughs of the pines they had been trimming that morning, the much older Andrew giving his little brother the advantage of a longer sword. In the photo, Charles sat atop the tractor, smiling down at them.

At least he remembered smiling. He picked up the photo for a closer look at his sun-faded expression. He could be *feeling* as happy as a lark, and yet his expression seemed never to change. Adele knew how to read him, thank God, and said his eyes smiled even if his lips didn't follow along. Dour, he thought, just like his taciturn, stiff-necked old grandfather.

Of all the damn traits to inherit, he thought shaking his head, setting the picture back amongst the others.

He had once asked Adele to put one of the photos away, but she had her own brand of stubbornness and let it be. And it should not have been painful to see twelve-year-old Alexander gently cradling Iris, his newborn niece, except for the fact that one of them had just lost his hero, the other her father.

The color was faded, but not so faded he couldn't see Alex's somber expression and the wisps of red hair above the baby's swaddled cherub face. Dark red hair, the very same shade as her uncle's, and her father's, whom she would never know.

"Charles?"

He glanced up, surprised to see his wife and to find that he was now holding the photo of Alexander and Iris.

"You were miles away," Adele said, resting her hand lightly on his shoulder.

"Miles and years." Setting the frame gently back in its place, Charles made an effort to smile, knowing very well she wouldn't find one in his eyes.

Chapter Two

"WELCOME TO MIDDLE SCHOOL!" said Miss MacMaster, after the announcements ended and seats were assigned. "I hope you've all had a great summer. I *also* hope you are ready for your first day of seventh grade and ready to get to work!"

Most of the class groaned at the word work as the teacher began handing out stacks of thick packets to the first student in each row.

When the last copy reached Iris Gibson, she saw the illustration of a large tree, each of its sprawling branches labeled with father and mother, grandmother and grandfather and so on, all the way up to the top.

"*Yes!*" Miss MacMaster insisted with a smile, "get to work and have fun with a special project. I know you're going to love it, so let's not waste any time!"

Iris groaned inwardly as very bad memories of fourth grade flooded back, along with an odd sinking feeling in her stomach. No one in her class had fewer blocks filled in on their family tree, and along with the

C minus, the teacher had called her family tree a *shrub* and laughed.

And then the whole class had laughed.

Iris never knew what her mother said to the principal the next morning, but the teacher wasn't laughing when she later apologized to Iris. It wasn't really something she wanted to go through again.

She didn't want to tell this teacher why she didn't know anything about her family. *"My father died before I was born. We don't know his family and my mother doesn't want to know hers."* Well, she thought, glancing at the teacher, at least Miss MacMaster didn't look like the kind of teacher who would laugh at a student.

Just one more way to be different, she thought, flipping through the pages.

It wasn't enough that her mother had given her a granny name or that she had inherited her father's dark red hair that her teachers loved but her classmates always made fun of. She could be sitting next to a kid with neon pink or bright blue hair and *she* would be the one to be teased.

She did, at least, like her dark blue eyes and she wasn't the shortest one in class anymore. Last year one of her friends told her she was *really* pretty, at least after you looked at her for a while, whatever that meant. Her mother said she would be "striking" one day, another description that really confused her.

"This semester..." Miss MacMaster paused, glancing around the room to make sure they all had packets in front of them, stopping briefly at Iris and frowning slightly. Iris straightened up in her seat.

"This semester Literature and Social Studies are teaming up so that we can spend time learning in depth about one of the countries of our family origin. Most of us have branches to our family trees that come from several different countries or regions of the United States. For this project, however, we are going to choose *one*. You will read books about this area and choose a display project, such as a diorama, a poster or create your very own coat-of-arms!"

As she talked, she gestured towards the maps on the walls, books on the shelves, and examples of projects of former students along the counter at the back of the room. "We'll go through the packet today and tomorrow because there are many elements to this project, and I want you all to do well *and* enjoy it!"

"Yes..." she said, pausing to glance at her seating chart, "Justin?"

"My whole family has just lived around here...well...forever, my Dad always says."

"Excellent! You will be very intrigued by the local history of Southern California. We often take for granted what is right in our own neighborhood."

Iris looked out at the dusty old oak tree in the sunbaked courtyard as the class asked questions or talked about the far-away countries their parents or grandparents had emigrated from, and then down at the branches of the tree on the assignment in front of her and began to wonder about her grandparents for the first time in a long while.

She took a deep breath and raised her hand.

"Yes, Iris?"

"I had to do something like this in fourth grade. We don't know very much about our family..."

Miss MacMaster regarded her thoughtfully, long enough so Iris could feel her face getting warm.

"Thank you, Iris. That is a very good point. Not all families know about their ancestors, for many different reasons. That is why we are showing you how to discover your family origins and the fascinating things about the places and cultures that we all come from. This project is not so much about how many blocks you can fill in on your family tree, or the specific details you know or don't know about your ancestors, so don't worry about that. It's about learning something meaningful about one part of your heritage.

"Your last name, for instance, Gibson, has origins in the same country as mine, MacMaster. It certainly doesn't sound the same, though, does it? Does anyone know which country?" She glanced around the room and seeing no hands up, pointed to a country high on the world map. "Our names are both of Scottish origin. Ever heard of Bonnie Prince Charlie? Ever heard of the Loch Ness Monster? *Scotland* is a country very rich in history and legend, tradition and exciting imagery. And redheads," she added, laughing, putting a hand up to her own bright auburn hair that was loosely bunched high on her head, some escaping in unruly curls. Iris cringed as some of the kids laughed and all heads in the class swiveled from the teacher to her.

After a few more questions, the teacher went over the assignment page by page. After the bell, Miss MacMaster called out to her, "Iris, I have lots of information on Scotland. If you want, stop by after school!"

Out in the hallway, Iris studied her schedule to find the room number of her next class, while also trying to remember the direction of her locker. She was immediately caught up in the tide of kids doing the same thing, most of them at the top of their lungs.

Three tries of her combination later she was finally in and reaching for her math book when someone crashed into the locker next to her.

"Watch it, you little..." said a voice far over Iris's head to the short, skinny kid who had clearly made it mad. She tipped her head back to see an older student towering overhead.

"Get out of here, Gil, he didn't do anything to you!" said one of the girls Iris recognized from her Lit class, Ashley, who stepped between the two boys.

"Yes, Mr. Moran, you don't want to renew your relationship with the in-school suspension room on your very first day," said one of the teachers, pointing down the hall. "Do try not to initiate any altercations on your way to class. Two more minutes, people! Let's try to be on time!"

"You know that jerk?" Iris asked the girl, once the kid between them had scurried off in the other direction.

"Which one?" she asked, glancing at the teacher and meeting Iris's eyes with a smirk. Ashley looked down at Iris's schedule. "Come on, we're in the same class again."

Gibson, she discovered, was a family name associated with the Clan Buchanan and from an area called the Lowlands in Scotland. But that was her father's name and as her mother reminded her, when Iris finally broached the subject several days later, she had no information about his family.

"I can't believe we have to go through this again! I know it's not your fault, but I told you before, Iris," Jennifer said, over the commotion made by her two four-year-old stepbrothers, "when we had to deal with this two years ago."

"Three," Iris said, as she wiped the spaghetti sauce from Harry's face and lifted him off his booster seat.

"Three, that your father came from somewhere up near Sacramento and I met his family only once. Which I can barely remember because it was right after Andrew died, and just after you were born."

Jennifer paused to do the same for Heath, shooed both boys out to their dad in the living room and sighed in relief in the now quiet kitchen. She turned to Iris with a tired smile.

"You're so much like Andrew, you know, with

that gorgeous hair of yours and those big blue eyes... even your square chin. Did you know that means you can be very stubborn?" Before Iris could say anything, her mother looked away and changed the subject. "I was so glad to get married and change my last name from Browne—how boring is *that*? Still, honey, I could at least give you a little bit more information on my side of the family."

Iris did know a little bit of that history and wondered, for the hundredth time, why her mom didn't want to see her own mother. She couldn't be *all* that bad, could she? Seeing her stepfather's parents hug and make a fuss over Heath and Harry made her miss having her own grandparents even more.

She missed her mom sometimes, too, the way things used to be when weekends were spent doing things together like hiking in the Santa Monica Mountains or roller skating at the park. Jennifer would watch movies with Iris and her friends and they always cooked breakfast and dinners together.

They had met Eric at their grief support meetings. Eric had attended another group for a year after his wife had left him and the twins, and had only recently joined their group. Jennifer had been involved since Iris was very young. They still attended each week, though her mother was now more of a facilitator than an attendee. Since there were rarely any other kids her age at these meetings, Iris either did homework or babysat, which was how she met her future stepbrothers.

After meeting Eric, their time was interrupted more and more by their dates and his visits, but she liked Eric well enough, even though their lives had changed a lot after her mom married him. Her mother's name changed which made her feel a little left out, a little different, too, when she saw her mom and Eric and the boys together, all four of them with their dark brown hair.

Eric was nice to her, and even told her Mom that Iris *had* to help them find the new apartment so it felt like home to her. He helped her with homework and showed her how to do things like fixing the chain on her bike. She would *never* admit it but agreed with her Mom and her friends that he was handsome. Iris liked the way he smiled, the way she could see it in his eyes.

He always invited her to watch *really* old movies with them, and mimicked the actors and said things like, "Frankly, my dear, I don't give a damn" when she complained about taking out the garbage or something. Every now and then she would get him back, like when he asked her to do the dishes and she said, "I'll think about that tomorrow!"

"Can I see our birth certificates, though, so I can put all the names and dates in my research packet?" she asked, clearing the dishes from the table as her Mom put the leftovers away. She looked over when Jennifer didn't respond right away. "Mom?"

"I can tell you that much, honey."

Iris wiped off the table and countertops as her mother started to rinse the dishes and load the dishwasher. "Ashley had hers at school today, and copies of her Mom and Dad's. They were all *super* pretty and from different countries –even Ashley's. She was born in Germany when her Dad was in the Army."

Ashley said her mom might give in to peer pressure. But it *was* true, all the kids in class had been telling stories and showing old photographs and fancy certificates all week.

"I want to see mine. Please?"

"See what?" Eric asked, coming into the kitchen.

"Family birth certificates for my project."

"*All right*, Iris!" her mom answered impatiently.

Eric made a funny face at Iris, grabbed what he came in for and left, and Jennifer added in a softer tone, "If I can find them, that is. I think I know where they are after the last move.

"But," she added, turning away from loading the dishwasher and shook her finger at Iris, "don't even think about pestering me about seeing your grandmother like you did last time. I wish things were different, but they're not." Jennifer smiled and she leaned over to plant a kiss on Iris's forehead. "I love you too much to subject you to her."

"But…"

"I'll do my best to find the certificates to give you something for your project, but promise me, Iris, please don't get anything else into your head."

Iris nodded. "Okay, but—"

Suddenly there was a loud crash in the other room followed by Eric's swearing.

"Okay. But don't you love me enough not to subject me to those two?"

Jennifer started to laugh, but seeing that Iris wasn't laughing herself, sighed instead, "Well, they sure love you in their four-year-old boy kind of way," she paused before adding, "I meant to tell you earlier, but we need you to watch them again tomorrow."

"*Again*? Mom, it was every day last week!"

"Shh! I'm sorry, but Margie has jury duty one more week and Jean can only watch them until four. Just a couple hours after school, okay?"

Iris wanted to say no, but the expression on her mom's face stopped her. Jennifer looked tired, really tired, with shadows under her eyes she had never noticed before. Iris knew she didn't like her job processing people's insurance in the windowless little office at the hospital, and had heard her say more than once that sitting in front of a computer all day made her tired.

Iris couldn't think of a more depressing job.

Chapter Three

USELESS. THAT'S WHAT I AM, Charles thought, closing the bedroom door.

Now a week since their visit to the doctor, and each day he seemed to be able to walk fewer steps and lift fewer pounds before weariness and breathlessness made him stop even the easiest chore.

He couldn't watch Adele anymore. She was worried and when she was worried she worked. Not serenely at one task or another as she usually did, but flitting between her dusting or painting or cooking or baking until it wore him out just watching her.

And that's about all it took these days, he thought, shaking his head. Once he would have worked away his own anxiety by pruning, culling out the weak or deformed among the perfect ornamentals, chopping firewood. Now, if he could do any of those things, neither of them would be anxious.

He lay on the bed, watching dust motes dancing in the afternoon sun shining through the gap in the old curtains she had made to match the patchwork quilt twenty years before. Just as well she was busy in the kitchen, as that would likely set her off on a whole new cleaning frenzy.

Useless, his mind repeated over and over as he sat up and opened the drawer of his bedside table to put away his watch. Too roughly, and the next thing he knew, it was overturned on the floor at his feet.

Sighing, again, he knelt to pick up the clutter from the drawer he hadn't looked deeply into for years, the spare change, odd receipts, old notes and a few broken pencils, two pocket knives he'd forgotten about and a broken belt buckle he'd meant to fix. And his rosary.

He threw it all back into the drawer and jiggled it back into place, but paused before closing the drawer. He took out the blue satin pouch with the rosary Adele had given him just before he was confirmed into the Catholic Church.

The small silver beads between the larger of deep, cobalt blue were tarnished, but not the small crucifix. Holding them gently in his cold, callused hands took him back to Inverness, in old Saint Mary's Church, when she had knelt beside him and prayed the rosary with him for the first time.

He was as religious as the next man, he had told her once, depending on who that next man was. She hadn't found that as amusing as he had, but then he had grown up around his strict Presbyterian grandfather, a close-minded old Calvinist if ever there was one. Once Charles had thought it was the religion that had made the old man grim and dour, but thinking back, Charles knew it had been the old man that made the religion grim and dour. His rigid hand-me-down principles and prejudices had all but annoyed any true faith out of Charles by the time he left home. In contrast, Adele was unreservedly connected to her faith, even the hierarchy and dogmatic folderol attached to it that he could never quite appreciate.

Ironic, Charles thought, that something so abhorrent to one believer is the salvation for another, and he often envied the certainty and comfort her faith brought to his wife. He had grumbled a bit, repeating some of his grandfather's prejudices about false gods and idolatry, watered down considerably, of course. Truthfully, he could never see what the fuss was about one side or the other, why there had to be sides, or judgments about how a person wanted to relate to God.

Still, he converted to Catholicism without hesitation, even knowing it would not be a condition to marry her. He had never told her that he would have donned a sikke and whirled like a Dervish if it meant she would marry him.

His own faith in the Almighty was nurtured out among the trees. He wasn't sure if that made him a Druid or not, which may very well have been preferable to Roman Catholicism to some, but it connected him to the Almighty in a way being inside a church, any church, or kneeling with a string of beads never could.

He glanced over to the small, pine prie-dieu he

had made for her many years before to provide earthly comfort to her evening prayers, and then down at the beads. The momentary impulse to kneel and pray was replaced with a gruff snort of a laugh at the alarm it would cause Adele at the sight of him kneeling with rosary in hand.

Chapter Four

IRIS CAME HOME FROM school to find a large envelope on the counter, a bright green sticky note from her stepdad on top. "Here are the certificates you asked for! Have fun—but your mom says practice first!"

Iris groaned. Her mother was determined she would get her thirty minutes on the violin each and every day and seemed to know whenever she didn't.

"You're a natural," her mom would always say, and Iris would answer, "If I'm a natural, why do I have to practice?"

Strange that Eric left them for her, she thought, but he did work from home sometimes, and she knew he was still setting up his office after they had moved in two months before.

Their new apartment was much bigger than their last place, even her room was much bigger and the walls were already painted a soft buttery yellow.

Iris hadn't thought anything of it when Jennifer started to use the same old cartoon character curtains and comforter, but Eric took Iris shopping for brand new, and at a *nice* place, too.

Drawn to two completely different patterns, Eric had said, "Why not a mix of both?"

"Plaid *and* flowers?" her mother had asked when they returned, one eyebrow raised, when peering into the package and back at the two of them.

Once the new linens were washed and dried free of wrinkles and in her room, even her mom admitted the combination was lovely.

Curtains and comforter were plaid of a deep, dark blue with narrow bands of red, white, green and yellow, and the bed sheets and pillow cases were white and dotted with small sprigs of flowers—daffodils, roses, lilies and even irises. Sheer panels with the same wildflower pattern fluttered at the open windows. She thought her bedroom was the prettiest she had ever seen.

Smiling, Iris picked up her violin, remembering the first few nights when she hadn't even wanted to turn off her bedside lamp and close her eyes it was so pretty.

Thirty-one minutes later, she was sitting at the kitchen table opening the envelope.

She recognized her own and her mother's birth certificates immediately, but there were two others in a separate, smaller envelope that she had never seen before.

Her father's birth certificate! With his cute little inky footprints on the back! Her grandfather's name was Charles Stewart Gibson, almost the same as her father's, she noticed. Her grandmother's name was Adele Eleanor MacIntyre. The second certificate was for her father's baptism just a few days after his birth at a church called Saint Catherine's.

"Well, at least you have two more blocks than you did this morning," said Ashley, when she came over to spend the night. "And you know they're Catholic, like we are. What are you? Are you and your mom Catholic?"

Iris shook her head and looked to make sure her mom wasn't near. "We're not anything. Mom said that church is… well, it has something to do with her mom. Anything that has to do with her mom she doesn't like."

Ashley started to say something, but then seemed to change her mind and pointed to the name of the town on the birth certificate. "Well, you know what town he was born in and that might help you find out more. Sometime you can come over and we'll Google them until we find something!"

The very first time Iris had been at Ashley's house, Mr. Ramirez had joked that Ashley's middle name ought to be 'Google' since she looked up everything for everyone and had become something of an expert. Now it was second nature for her to 'Google' everything.

Ashley's father was from the Philippines and she

had only a few more blocks than Iris on his side. Ashley's mother's family tree was on several huge sheets of paper taped together and onto the living room wall. "All the way back to the first settlers in the Canadian Maritimes," she had told Iris, matter-of-factly. *Wherever that was*, Iris thought, but had felt envious, seeing Ashley's name in the tiny block at the bottom of the page near the floor.

Iris, on the other hand, still had only three generations on her family tree and didn't even have access to a computer, since her mother had recently banned her from using Eric's again because it had the temerity to crash the day after she used his old laptop. *He* didn't seem to blame her and even hinted that they might get a family computer for Christmas. But that would be too late.

"Have you chosen the novel you're going to read, Iris?" Miss MacMaster asked, setting two books on Iris's desk. "These might be good for your project."

"No, not yet," Iris said, looking up from darkening the lines around the few boxes on her family tree and glancing at the book titles. She quickly shook her head. "My life's too boring. There would never be anything in *my* history about princes or being kidnapped."

"I'm not so sure about that," said Miss MacMaster, smiling, crouching next to the desk. "Look at this, Iris, see the first and middle names of your grandfather? Now, look at this book – same name! *This* Charles Stuart was a prince, "Bonnie Prince Charlie" he was called, and he has a very interesting history. I'm sure your grandfather has an interesting story as well, but even if you aren't able to know the facts, you can imagine and invent a story for yourself."

Iris tapped her pencil on her chart. "Can I imagine and invent the rest of this family tree?"

Miss MacMaster laughed, but kindly, and touched Iris lightly on the shoulder as she did. "Well, that is one part of this assignment we don't want to mix fact and fiction! But remember, Iris, it doesn't matter how many of those blocks you fill in, so *please* don't worry about that. For the rest of the project, you have a lot more facts than you realize. For your display project, you may want to consider creating your very own coat of arms." She stood up, adding, "Let me show you."

They went to the resource shelf and Miss MacMaster pulled out a large book, its cover bright with red dragons and blue eagles and golden shields. She flipped through several pages before stopping to point out several examples. Iris looked at the shields with their vibrant colors and illustrations of knights in armor and strange animals. "Just like I explained in the packet, the figures, lines and colors in your coat of arms need to be accurate, meaning they need to truly represent your name and family heritage, but that still leaves a lot of room for creativity. You might want to separate your shield in quarters, using each section for a different aspect of your identity."

The teacher pointed out specific examples, and smiled as she pointed out a bright blue shield covered with golden fleurs-de-lis.

"You could make it as simple as this quartered shield, or use these narrow chevrons if you wanted a different design. In one section, you might use a fleur-de-lis to signify your first name, a cross or perhaps even a dove to illustrate the meaning of your middle name, with symbols from the coats of arms for your last name and your mother's that might go well in the other two.

"See, what did I tell you? So many possibilities and we've barely scratched the surface!"

"Can I ask you some questions for my project, Mom?"

Iris knelt by the coffee table and pulled out her homework folder, and scanned the list of questions. Her mom glanced up from the basket of clothes she was folding.

"What kind of questions? I really don't know much more than I've already told you—"

"Why did you choose my first name?"

"Oh." Her mom stopped, surprised by the simple question. "Oh, well, that's easy. Irises were your father's favorite flower—didn't I ever tell you that?"

Iris shook her head, "And Christine?"

"My good friend was with me in the hospital, all through the time of my labor and your birth. She insisted on talking about Andrew." Iris heard her mom's voice go shaky before Jennifer paused, "even though it was painful for both of us, she said she wanted to keep him 'present'. She was a bit of a new age spirit, was Bethany, but I remember her saying, at some quiet moment, that Andrew was the most Christian man she had ever met..."

"Oh," Iris said, her own voice feeling shaky, and looked down at her list again. "Why did your parents choose your names, and did you have a nickname?"

Startled again by the harmless question, her mother laughed. "Oh, well, I don't know. Jennifer was probably the most popular name at the time or something like that. Ann was for my grandmother. No nicknames until I met your father. My mother did *not* approve of nicknames."

"What did my father call you?"

"Jenny. And you've heard Eric – Jen, Jenny and sometimes even Jennifer..."

"Who is the oldest relative you've ever met?

"That would be the same grandmother – my mother's mother."

"Did she live in Seattle, too?" Iris had stopped reading from her list.

"No. She just visited from the East Coast a few times. The last time, I think I was about your age."

"Why? Did she get sick or something?"

Jennifer shrugged, and folded the last few towels. "Probably because my mother was a raging ... witch towards her. I never understood why, really, she always seemed nice to me."

"Where did she live? Did you ever go visit her?"

"She lived in Connecticut somewhere. And no, honey, we never went anywhere to visit anyone when I was young. Now, I better put this stuff away and get on with my other chores or I'll never get to bed tonight." She picked up the basket of clothes and headed towards the bedroom. "Maybe Eric can help you when he gets home."

"But Mom…" Iris said, a list of questions still to be asked and answered. As the door closed between them, she was angry at both her mom and at hearing the quiver in her voice. "It's not like math, you know…."

Iris reached for her phone to call Ashley.

"I wonder what it is about her past she doesn't want to talk about," Ashley said when Iris paused to take a breath.

"It's everything in her past she doesn't want to talk about!" Iris was finding it hard to yell in a whisper. "It doesn't matter what I ask her, how I ask her. It's always been like that—and Eric isn't really part of my family. Why should I ask him?"

"Stepparents *do* go on the family tree, Iris," Ashley said, "The packet says that you can use any –"

"Oh, all right!" Iris closed her phone with a snap and stared down at her homework, already feeling bad for hanging up on Ashley. She sighed, and by the time she had finished texting an apology, Eric was home.

After he hung his jacket in the hall closet and

kicked off his shoes, he stopped and looked down at her work spread out across the table.

"How's the project coming along?"

"Not great," she answered bluntly, not caring if she sounded rude. "Mom wondered if *you* could help me, maybe... since... well, you know..." she stopped, her voice faltering.

"Be glad to, Iris," he said, without hesitation, pulling off his tie. "Tell you what, you grab a soda for me, and I'll go change —"

"Right now?" she asked, surprised.

"Sure, why not?"

It wasn't a fight, really, Iris thought, hearing their voices when she came back into the living room, slowly, carrying the glass which was nearly full to the brim. The straw kept floating up to the surface no matter how many times she pushed it down.

"Of course I don't mind!"

"Shh!" Iris heard her mom hushing him, but it wasn't like he was yelling or anything. Still, he lowered his voice, so she crept closer to the bedroom door to hear.

"Iris is in the kitchen. And she wants to know about your family and Andrew's family—*her* family—"

"*You* are her family now."

"She doesn't need to know everything you went through when you were young, Jen, she just needs to fill in some blanks on a homework assignment."

"You don't understand!" Now her mom raised her voice, but Eric didn't try to hush her. "I don't want to talk about my family. *Ever.*"

In the long pause that followed, Iris knew it was time to creep back to the kitchen before one of them caught her listening.

"I'm just worried," Eric said finally, his voice soft and sort of sad, "that if you don't give her something soon she'll start searching for answers on her own."

When the bedroom door opened, Iris was just slinking down beside the coffee table, homework open in front of her. Eric stretched out on the sofa, and said. "Fire away, kid!"

Chapter Five

"I WAS THINKING, INSTEAD of closing, we might ask Jerry and Daniel to take over completely this year. If you wanted, you could still be out in your wee shop."

Adele looked up, one arched eyebrow raised, from adding more pepper to her beef stew.

"The doctor..."

"The doctor be damned, Adele," Charles said, taking his turn with the pepper shaker. "Just because I'm useless, doesna mean everything has to come to a halt."

He watched as she sipped her hot tea, enjoying the fiery heat of the combination with the peppery soup. She set down the delicately painted cup in its matching saucer—the autumn oak leaf pattern, to match the change of tablecloth and napkins, and the change in the weather. Temperatures were falling and color was creeping into the oak trees and the young maple tree outside the kitchen window.

"And when the old tractor has its usual mid-season fit and you're the only one who can ever fix the thing? When you've heard we've run out of baling net or that one of the elves *canna* tell the difference between a Fr-raser fir and a Douglas fir? Not to mention the ladies who look forward to flirting with you every year?" she smiled at his expression. "You could sit patiently in the house, taking naps and watching 'It's a Wonderful Life?"

He answered with the low Scottish growl that expressed so many different feelings and opinions, he knew Adele had long ago taken to applying the one that she wanted given the circumstances.

"*I* was wondering if you wanted to go home for the holidays," she said.

"Home? To Inverness?" Most of his kin still lived in and around a tiny village near the larger town.

"And why not? It has been eighteen years since our last trip to Scotland."

Another growl, but this one in good humor.

"Do you happen to remember what I did during that last trip, Adele? Repaired ancient plumbing, and replaced missing roof slates and listened to you and Alexander complain of cold, for all it was June."

"Well, you wouldn't *have* to work and we could stop in Pringles for a few new jumpers before — "

"Winter in Scotland, in a two-hundred-year-old house with no central heating? You'd need to be mummy wrapped in lamb's wool and goose down not to complain!"

"But..." she started to interrupt.

"Bad weather, crowded airports, delayed

flights...nay, Adele, we'll bide," he reached out and took her hand. "Plan a trip for spring or summer, if you like, but for now I'd rather be bored and warm in my own home. You can do all the things you say you never have time for at Christmas, and while you do, I'll try my best to get better and not drive you crazy in the waiting."

A hard autumn frost still sparkled on the ground, the crisp morning air heartbreakingly fresh with the scent of balsam fir. Charles could tell the direction of the breeze by the scent of evergreen it carried. Northeast, this morning, he thought, breathing deep and looking at the sky.

All the better for Daniel and his friends who would be along soon, to start working in the lower tracts. Opening for the season or not, work still needed to be done and the boys could all use the money as there wasn't a lot of work in the area this time of year.

Without planning a route, he walked along the fence line where a crop of hardy nasturtium vines still grew beneath the short row of sycamore trees along the old wooden rails. He plucked some of the late orange and yellow blossoms, remembering how he had once shown the boys how to nip off the end of the spur to taste the honey nectar inside. Now he munched the entire blossom, enjoying the spicy sweetness.

From the fence, he turned left into the balsams and crossed through into the long row of blue spruce and then walked along the tract of the Scots pines, his own sentimental favorites, reminders of home and family, and his early days in Forestry school in the Highlands which led to meeting Adele.

Charles greeted the trees, touching the tips of the boughs in passing and felt like a dried up old sponge set in a puddle, soaking up the milieu around him; the aroma of rich damp soil and the tang of evergreens, the warmth of the sun on his back and cool breeze on his face, the scratch of sharp spruce or tickle of pine needles on his palms.

Still, he hadn't meant to venture out so far and knew he'd better make his way home. Adele had promised to pick up a new movie for them to watch.

Threatened was more like it, Charles thought.

Like an evil spell cast in one of those recent movies, frustration and powerlessness sometimes overwhelmed him when he watched stories of hero's fighting battles to protect their women and land from evil and injustice. Worse still were the stories of strong women, fighting their own battles without, or in spite of, the presence of some weak-bodied or feeble-minded man in their lives.

Bless her, though, he knew she enjoyed the distraction and thought he did as well. She never saw the connection when she was scolding him an hour later when he tried to do something that was now beyond his strength.

Two days before, the doctor had delivered a walker.

Puddock.

The Gaelic expression crossed Charles's mind with amusement, but beneath was anger and a deep sense of betrayal. Dr. Alford had been a friend and neighbor for twenty years. Was it too much to expect some other result from six months of the man's ministrations than the clumsy metal contraption that now stood waiting for him to grow weaker?

But, seeing that the walker remained unused when Charles went for his walk, he knew it would be inadvisable to be out and away from the house when Adele returned. At least she couldn't nag him about the damn pills since he had taken his dose early before leaving the house.

Turning back, he saw a gnarly old root extending into the path. A wonder he hadn't tripped on the bloody thing on his way down, he thought, automatically reaching over to pull it out and toss it to the side.

Another of the damnable hot flashes flared, followed by waves of dizziness and nausea. He rested, hands on knees, took a few deep breaths to clear his head and tried again. He gripped the root with both hands and pulled harder, until, rather than pulling it out, he had the disconcerting sensation that the old root was pulling him down.

Adele had taken one look at him when she got home and called the doctor. Unfortunately for Charles,

Doctor Alford still made house calls.

"No, it's not the wrong medicine, Charles," said the doctor with exaggerated patience. Making a dismissive gesture, he put his stethoscope away and stood to leave. "Your body has simply adjusted to the low dose and now it's time for a slight increase.

"On the positive side, I think you are starting to respond to the treatment and why you're starting to have more energy now and then."

"Why is it, then," Charles started, his jaw tight with anger, "you want me in that?" He nodded towards the wheelchair now parked near the door.

"You need to preserve what strength you do have, Charles. This may be the most difficult, but it is also the most crucial point in your recovery. It's more important than ever to take it easy. I know you're impatient, both of you, but give yourself this time."

Charles didn't answer when the doctor said his farewells, nor did he answer Adele when she asked about lunch. He stood up on his own two feet and walked to the bedroom.

"Well, Charles, I wouldn't put anything past some of those characters on the commission." Sheriff Brent Abbott glanced around the diner and motioned towards the gossiping hostess for a refill. "Brad Porter and young Miss Kelly are hammering away on the subject at every meeting."

"We've said no to them three times during the

last six months. There's nothing they can do if we don't want to sell," said Charles.

"I just wish the Sierra Recreation Group had chosen to take their development plans elsewhere. This has unsettled a whole lot of folks in the area." The sheriff gave up on the hostess and went for his own refill. When he came back, he changed the subject and shared some of the lighter local gossip.

Charles didn't know why the rumor about Kelly Alford and George Grant being seen together outside DJ's Bar was so disturbing. The doc's daughter was a prissy miss and social climber, and one of those on the commission pushing hardest for them to sell. George was a dirty blue jeans and old tee shirt kind of guy, who, incidentally, had it in for the Gibson's ever since Charles had exposed the shoddy work and shady business practices that finished his small excavation company years before. What they could possibly have in common, he didn't know.

"So, the other local gossip is that Adele has you grounded. What did you do, set out to prune the lower forty or something?"

Charles gave the sheriff a good-natured growl and shook his head at the harried young waitress who finally made the rounds to offer refills. Too much coffee made him jumpy these days, along with too many other things.

Charles told him the long version of his adventures out in the trees, starting with his cockiness at being out of doors without his worrying wife for the first time in weeks, his defeat in the tug-of-war with the old pine root, and waking up with the faces of Daniel, Sean and Hamid looking down at him.

Daniel nearly had him into the house when Adele drove in. It hadn't taken her keen eye long to detect the signs of his tumble onto the path. She even knew how far away from the house he had been when she pulled blue spruce needles from his hair.

The sheriff laughed sympathetically and finished his coffee. He pushed back from the table and stood up. "Lift home?"

Charles shook his head. "Adele will be along soon. This is her way of keeping me off my feet and out of trouble."

"Well, I wish her luck with *that*, my friend!"

After Brent left, Charles picked up the newspaper and looked at it without reading.

The Gibson's refusal to sell their property to grant access for a new recreational development near Clear Creek Reservoir was well known, but that had not stopped them from trying again and again. The early offers were laughable, easy to refuse not only because the amounts were insulting but because he and Adele were well, Alexander was still planning to come home and business had never been better.

With the offers now beginning to approach the actual value of the place, and his health steadily failing, it made him wonder …

Chapter Six

"STEP-PARENTS *CAN* GO on the family tree, you know," Ashley repeated the next day, in the hall on their way to class, as though their call the night before hadn't been so rudely interrupted.

"I *know*," said Iris, ducking behind Ashley single file when a crowd of eighth graders swaggered down the hall, "but that's not the point!"

She was still angry at her mother, but it was more than that. She felt it was wrong, well, sort of disloyal to Andrew Gibson, to put her stepfather on her family tree.

"You like him, don't you?" Ashley asked, when Iris was next to her again, "Sarah can't stand her stepfather. She said he's always telling her off and making up new rules all the time."

Iris remembered when Eric asked her mom to marry him, and said that Iris had to give her approval, too, or it couldn't happen.

"Eric told me it was still my mom's job to make my rules and still his job to make rules for the twins."

Iris paused and laughed, "After Mom left the room, he said it would also be his job to help me *bend* Mom's rules."

Iris had seen with her own eyes that they were in love, and she did like Eric. The boys were little terrors, sometimes, but she liked the way he corralled them when they got out of hand, most of the time by playing with or cuddling them and saved the scolding and punishments for big things... like when Harry was trying to "help" and was underfoot in the kitchen and got too close to the stove or when Heath went running through the parking lot at the mall. He could laugh instead of scold, too, like when both boys immediately dived in and went swimming in the expanding pool of olive oil after Eric dropped the big plastic bottle on the pantry floor.

Once in class, when it was her turn on the computer, she remembered what he had said the night before when she shouldn't have been listening. *I'm just worried that if you don't give her something soon she'll start searching for answers on her own.* She entered her search term in the browser, not a heraldic image or a period in Scottish history, but a name. Her grandfather's, and she felt like she was on a brink of a major discovery about herself, with one click of a mouse...

She spent the rest of the class period looking at about a *thousand* of the over forty thousand websites about news broadcasters, football players and actors, and a lot of other people, and she didn't think any one of them was her grandfather. Ashley looked over her shoulder just before the bell rang.

"How's it going?"

"Not great—there are a *lot* of people in the world named Charles Gibson!"

Ashley rolled her eyes. "That's all you entered?

"I tried Charles Stewart Gibson, too. That was only thirty thousand—"

The bell rang and Iris logged out of the computer, defeated.

"On Friday, when you stay overnight, we'll do a *real* search!"

Iris knew Eric had helped her gain permission to spend the night with Ashley, too. Always before, Iris could have friends over but never spend nights away from home. He had made it a point for them to stay long enough to visit whenever they picked Ashley up or dropped her off so that her mom could meet Ashley's parents and see their home. Finally, Jennifer had reluctantly allowed Iris to accept an invitation for Thanksgiving weekend.

By Thanksgiving, Iris had read the books about the rebellious Scottish prince with the same names as her grandfather and had the foundations of her personalized coat-of-arms in place, but the family tree remained …well, a *shrub*, Iris admitted to herself.

For the holiday, they drove from Pasadena to Eric's parent's house in Burbank two towns over, without ever leaving the freeway.

Iris thought their house smelled funny and during their last visit, had sat in the backyard all day. Now a cold, drizzling rain was falling so there would be no escape outside today.

Just after sitting down to dinner in the old, dimly lit dining room, Iris was horrified when Eric's mother, Mavis, spooned a huge helping of stuffing on not only her stepbrother's plates but hers as well, stuffing with huge chunks of onions and mushrooms, and other brown bits she didn't even recognize. Now, not only would she have to eat hers to be polite, they would all have to listen to the boys whine about eating theirs all through dinner. As his mother reached for the candied yams, Eric stopped her with a request for something from the kitchen. As soon as the door closed, he winked at Iris, took her plate and scraped most of the stuffing onto his own.

Before his mother had a chance to serve anything to anyone else, Eric told them that Iris was researching her family tree.

"Family history! How interesting, Iris!" Mavis cried, finally sitting down and filling her own plate. "*My* family originally came from France, did you know that? We're descendants of the Count dee Leezore. He and his entire family were able to escape the Revolution –and the guillotine, I might add—and emigrated from France and went to Louisiana…"

Eric's father, Sydney, was rolling his eyes and shaking his head a lot, too. Iris noticed that Sydney never talked much at all.

"...and it wasn't but a year later that those pampered aristocrats were trudging their way over the Oregon Trail..."

Sydney winked at Iris and mouthed the word 'fifty' when Mavis wasn't looking. She went on through each successive generation until the twins, bored with all the talk, started yelling and throwing bits of their uneaten stuffing at one another, and all conversation about their aristocratic lineage ended with a scolding.

After dinner, Iris escaped to what Mavis called the "formal" living room and found a place where she could text in peace. She took an old encyclopedia off the shelf and was reading about heraldry and all the meanings of the different symbols, colors, and lines when her mom found her.

"Good hiding place, isn't it?" said Jennifer. "Nice room, too. Shame they don't use it."

"Probably because all the furniture is covered in plastic," Iris said, smacking the hard, clear vinyl as her mother sat down next to her.

"I'm so tired right now, I could rest on a board," Jennifer said, leaning back, sighing, and closing her eyes. "Those guys are all over the place tonight, wears me out just watching them. Learning anything new on your project?"

"I'm trying to think of a good way to finish my coat-of-arms," Iris answered, surprised her mom asked about the assignment for a change. "All the colors and lines and symbols mean something, and I want to get them right."

Iris told her about the meanings of some of the symbols.

"And," she added, "a motto of one of the Browne families is Boldly and Faithfully and the motto of the Gibson family is Just and Faithful...almost the same."

"That's interesting," said her mom in a sleepy voice.

"What do they mean?"

Eyes still closed, her mom smiled just a little. "Well, faithful means to stay true to something you care about, similar to being honest, having loyalty and honor, I think. Bold is to be brave and courageous. And, to be just is to want justice and fairness. All very good things."

Iris wrote down her mother's explanation in her notes, then read a text from Ashley, and when she turned to ask her mom another question, Jennifer was asleep.

She took out the page with her family tree and looked at the seven lonely boxes filled in on that very big tree.

Out of curiosity, she took down another of the encyclopedias and found that Ruskin, Eric's last name, was a sept, a sort of branch, of the Clan Buchanan, just like Gibson!

She thought about the apartment and her room, how she was going to be able to spend the night with Ashley *and* how he had taken away that horrifying mound of stuffing on her plate, and well, maybe it *was* okay to add him to her family tree.

Her mother woke with a start when Eric came in, the boys squealing and climbing all over him.

"We've got to get these guys home to bed, and you, too by the look of things," he said, leaning down towards Jennifer, adding softly, "Shall we tell them our news?"

Jennifer, groggy from the short nap, looked at Iris as though she wanted to say something, over to Eric's parents who had just walked in the room, and then back to Eric. "Well, yes, I guess we'd better—"

He helped her to her feet and they stood facing the others.

Curious, Iris closed the encyclopedia and waited. They seemed even happier than when they announced their engagement.

'We're going to have a baby!"

While Sydney congratulated them quietly and Mavis made a big fuss over the boys being big brothers soon, Jennifer leaned over, hugged Iris and said, "I came in here to tell you, honey. I'm sorry I fell asleep...I meant to tell you first."

"Wow, Mom," was all Iris could say, and then Eric was tousling her hair and her mom was enveloped by her mother-in-law in congratulations and advice.

On the drive home, Iris looked through the sparkling raindrops on the window at the traffic and the billboards. Eric and Jennifer talked quietly in the front and the boys drifted off to sleep in their car seats on either side of her.

A baby. The whole idea made her a little queasy—she had started health class, after all.

And babies were great, like when she went to Ashley's and got to play with baby Sierra for a while. But one around the house, all the time?

"Wow," said Ashley, sympathetically.

The apartment was quiet and Iris was sure she was the only one awake when she called Ashley nearly two hours later. The reality was still sinking in.

"Yeah, I know."

"Well, you'll have more for your family tree, anyway. Did you find out anything else about your grandparents?" she added that quickly, somehow sensing the evil eye Iris gave her phone in the pause. "When you come over tomorrow we'll use every clue you have till we find something!"

Chapter Seven

THANKSGIVING AT THE FAMILY TREE was usually celebrated the weekend before the calendared holiday, because, as the day before the usual season-opening, none of them could afford to be over-stuffed and stupefied with tryptophan. It was another sign of the drastic change in the year's schedule to find the Abbots, Hendersons, and Lazarros at their table on Thanksgiving Day.

Their best china, silver, and linens were on the table, and the turkey Adele had just brought to him for carving was golden brown perfection. The same potluck dinner favorites were brought and shared, Adele's pumpkin pie ready to be enjoyed, and, Charles thought, too much of the same local news hashed over.

"I still think it's odd that a special planning commission was created just for the Sierra Recreation Group project," said Gail Henderson, passing the gravy boat into her husband Pete's gesturing hand. Gail had worked for the county in one capacity or another since high school and was always good for insight into its inner workings. "Sure, it will bring in huge revenues if it all goes through, but it's not so big a project that the regular commission can't handle it, especially because it is no way close to being a sure thing yet."

Brent Abbot reached across the table for another serving of his wife Fran's green bean casserole. "Special *favors* commission, is more like it," he said, chuckling.

"Brent!" Fran whispered sharply, nudging him in the ribs.

Charles knew that most of those around the table suspected that the person who had created the new office was having an affair with the new special planner, or was hoping to, though none of them would say it aloud, not with Daniel and his new girlfriend Lisa at the table. Some details of the local goings on, like special favors and blatant conflicts of interest, were better left unsaid in a certain setting.

"That's Kelly's job," Lisa said, chewing a morsel of something she had found to eat that was non-GMO, gluten, sugar, and milk free at their table. "She's been so nice to me lately."

"Just don't take any make-up tips from her," said Daniel, grimacing at the thought as he reached for the stuffing. "I think she puts it on with a trowel."

Lisa was the only one not to smile, snort or laugh out loud at the comment. Even Adele raised an eyebrow, Charles noticed. Kelly Alford was not known for her subtlety, especially in the application of beauty enhancers. When he wasn't annoyed with her, Charles was sad that the girl felt the need to be so made up, dress so provocatively and always be scheming to have more.

Lisa glared at Daniel but he was still reloading his plate and oblivious to the look she was sending his way.

"Kelly does give me good advice. She's even taking me Black Friday shopping in Sacramento tomorrow."

The lad didn't seem to get the hint and made a few more uncomplimentary remarks, including the observation that she was a scheming bit—when Jerry interrupted by asking his son to refill his coffee cup. Daniel grinned, finally getting the message. Adele tactfully steered the conversation in a new direction as Daniel refilled everyone's coffee and brought hot water for Gail and Adele's tea.

If Daniel hadn't any doubts about dating Lisa before, he should now, Charles thought, and he knew that Jerry was worried about his son, who was clearly infatuated with the pretty girl.

"You were born and raised in California, weren't you, Adele? How did you meet and marry this handsome Scot?" Gail Henderson asked later, winking at Charles as she cut and served pumpkin pie.

Charles girded himself for the teasing as Adele paused for a moment, remembering, "A friend of mine, Marianne, had the idea that we should go to Europe for a semester of college. I had heard about an art college in Inverness, and given our own roots in the Highlands, my father was all for me having the experience.

"In the end, my friend only lasted part of a semester—she was homesick and always complaining of the cold! I was, too, but I'd met Charles and stayed for over a year."

"But *how* did you meet, Adele?" Fran persisted, "did Charles sweep you off your feet?"

"He most certainly did," Adele said, adding with a smile, "although it was quite a *slow* sweep at the beginning. Charles had seen me at some gathering, but I hadn't noticed *him* yet. He found out I had a booth at a small Christmas art fair, a fundraiser for the local Catholic church. He came by three times and bought three of my hand-painted ornaments before he worked up the courage to ask me out to dinner." She turned her smile on him, "I've never told you, but if you had come back for a fourth, I would have asked *you* on a date!"

Charles vividly remembered that day, over forty years before, when it did take him repeated attempts to buck up his courage to ask her on that date. "Best decision I ever made," he said, amused to remember his love-struck timidity. He had come to believe in that gut instinct, to listen to that inner voice that had him returning to her table until he'd finally found his own voice and asked her out.

Charles remembered as Adele explained that it was her father that brought her home. Her mother had died some years before, and when her father became ill there was no one else to tend to him or the place. "Charles and I stayed in touch through a constant flow of letters and a few rare and very expensive telephone calls. After Charles finished school, my father and I traveled back for the wedding and then we all returned to California a few weeks later."

"The place was an apple orchard, wasn't it? Why the change to Christmas trees?" Brent Abbot asked, covering his second piece of pumpkin pie with a large dollop of whipped cream.

Charles was glad to veer the conversation from romance to arboriculture.

"The old man's health was failing along with the old apple trees," Charles said, "I had just finished my internship with the Forestry Commission, working with the reforestation program, and made the suggestion to replace the older sections with evergreens."

"My father was so relieved to have a strong and competent hand to help," said Adele, "even though he was sentimental about the family history and tradition of growing apples, he loved the idea of a Christmas tree farm. He'd inherited the apples when his father died, and truly loved the place but just never had a feel for the work that needed to be done." Charles heard the slight tremor in her voice as she remembered her father.

Bradford MacIntyre had never meant to take on the running of the apple farm started by his grandfather in the 1850's. Adele's father was a scholar who taught history at a small college back east until his retirement coincided with his own father's death. Brady meant well, but it was for good reason that Adele's grandfather had once despaired about the future of the farm. But Brady and Charles had taken a swift liking to one another, and he had trusted Adele and Charles to take over.

Adele had spent a good part of her youth at the farm and was bonded closely with both the land and the family business. She was an artist at heart, but Charles knew Adele could have put the business back on track all on her own if she'd had to. Hopefully, Charles thought, she wouldn't need to worry about that anytime soon.

Chapter Eight

"WOW!"

Iris and Ashley said together at the results of Ashley's Google search. They used the computer while Ashley's little sisters watched *Rudolph the Red Nosed Reindeer* on the big screen at the other side of the living room.

Ashley clicked onto the first site, a recent article from a Sacramento newspaper, in which there was just a brief mention of her grandparents.

> *"Among the most notable of the tree farms out in the Gold Country is 'The Family Tree' Christmas Tree Farm, a few miles north of Placerville, owned and operated by Charles and Adele Gibson. This renowned holiday venue will be closed for its first season since opening due to the illness of Mr. Gibson. The family hopes to reopen next season."*

"A Christmas tree farm! How cool is *that!*"

Ashley printed out the article and went to the next site.

"Wow!"

The opening page of The Family Tree Christmas Tree Farm website was a beautiful graphic of an elegantly decorated Christmas tree.

Each sparkling ornament was a link to different sections of the site. A large red ball with a green, red and gold plaid band around it was the link to the history of the farm. Owned by Iris's grandmother's family in the days of the Gold Rush, it had at first been a cattle ranch, later an apple orchard, and became a Christmas tree farm after the Gibson's were married.

Clicking on a candy cane opened a gallery of family pictures. Iris could barely breathe and was pointing and gaping soundlessly at the screen while Ashley read captions aloud and continued to print.

In the first, her grandfather Charles looked grimly into the camera, but her grandmother Adele was smiling radiantly next to him. The color photo showed her long, dark red hair, *exactly* the same as Iris's. Several more photos in a timeline of clearing and establishing the Christmas tree farm included two red-haired young boys planting, pruning and cutting trees. Andrew and Alexander—her father and her uncle! She had an uncle! He was a lot smaller than her dad in the pictures. How much younger was he, she wondered?

A revolving silver Christmas tree led to the contact information where a paper chain garland spelled out 'Closed for the Season' along the top of the

page. But there was still an address, telephone number
and an e-mail, even a map! If she could have, Iris
would have crawled right through the computer screen
and didn't even want Ashley to close it when they had
read every page.

"It's printing, Iris!" Ashley hissed, after getting
the ten-minute warning from her mom. "Let's go to
some other pages before Mom tells us to shut down!"

The last site Ashley clicked on was a San
Francisco newspaper article from several months
earlier, about county commissioners and land
developers that neither she or Ashley understood, but
Ashley printed it anyway.

"What does em...eminent domain mean?" Iris
asked, scanning the article as it printed.

"I don't know, but I'll look it up next." Ashley
entered the new search words. "Whatever it is, it
doesn't sound good," she said, after reading Wikipedia.
"It sounds like the government can take people's
property if they need it for something else. What does
that article say about your grandparent's place?"

"Umm...It says that 'even established and
flourishing properties like Ginger's Steakhouse and The
Family Tree may be at risk if the commissioners give in
to the influence of big money.'"

Ashley said, "Well, it doesn't sound like
anything is really happening, but I'll print it out
anyway," and the last page had just finished printing
when Ashley's mom walked by as predicted and told
them to turn off the computer and join the family for

their movie.

Later, up in the top bunk in Ashley's room, Iris had the entire batch of papers in her hands, going through each one of them again and again until Ashley finally turned off the lights.

"Isn't my grandmother beautiful? She has the same color hair as me and my dad! And my grandfather – I hope he's all right, Ashley, do you think he's all right?"

"I don't know, but he sure looks like a grump in those pictures."

Iris wasn't listening. "A Christmas tree farm! *How cool is that*!" she repeated, giggling. "And I have an uncle! How old do you think he is now? I wonder if he still lives there. I can't wait to show all of this to Mom!"

After a long pause, Ashley said, "Do you think you should?

"Why not?" Iris asked, leaning down to look through the shadows towards her friend.

"New husband, new baby? You know how she is, maybe she *has* known about them, but she doesn't want *you* to know about them. Maybe Eric would have a big problem with it, too. You never know, Iris. They could shut you down just like *that*!" Iris heard Ashley's fingers snap in the darkness.

"But she gave me the certificates, Ash. She couldn't have wanted to hide my grandparents from me forever if she gave me those!"

"You have to make contact first, e-mail them or call them, then it will be too late and your mom can't say no."

"Right now?"

"It's too late now!" Ashley scolded, "but tomorrow, for sure!"

By the time they were up, hurried out of the house to drop Iris at home before Ashley's gymnastics class, the warning was forgotten. Iris dropped the stack of printouts on the table where her mom and Eric were still having their morning coffee.

"Can I call them right now?" she asked, bubbling over about all she had discovered, almost dancing around the kitchen in anticipation.

Her mom was looking at the printout with the pictures, a strange expression on her face.

"Mom, they're my grandparents! They own a Christmas tree farm—did you ever know that? So how bad could they be?" She had stopped dancing and now stood still. "Please?"

"They may be your biological grandparents, Iris, but they are complete strangers! Besides the week you were born, I have never seen them, never spoken to them!" Her mom stood up and began to walk out of the kitchen, but abruptly turned back, adding with a vehemence she had never heard in her mother's voice, "And growing up on a Christmas tree farm may sound like a fairy tale, but I remember Andrew saying he was nearly worked to death on that place!"

"But, Mom—"

"No, Iris. Absolutely not."

Hearing her talk about her grandparents the same way she would talk about *real* strangers made Iris want to scream that Eric and those two nightmare boys of his had been strangers a year ago.

"It's just that it's hard to know who can be trusted, Iris," Eric said, as Iris was about to argue. "Since they *are* strangers, it's a good idea to let your Mom make the first call."

Eric was talking calmly, but Iris had seen him looking at her mother as though he didn't quite understand her reaction, either. "I'm sure if she feels okay about them, she'll let you get to know them. Maybe we can even visit sometime—"

"Please, Mom? Please let me write to them? The article said that my grandfather is sick. I want to find out if he's okay. I want to meet them before it's too late!"

But her mom gave her the look that said no amount of begging, pleading or whining would make her change her mind, and then turned and left the kitchen.

After a pause, Eric asked, "Are you okay, Iris?"

She nodded.

"I promised the boys a walk down to the park this morning. Want to go?"

Iris hesitated, but didn't want to be home alone with her mom so she nodded again.

"Bring along your research. I'd like to hear about it."

The winter day was warm and sunny after the recent rain, and a cool breeze carried the scent of nearby eucalyptus trees. The boys ran to a seesaw and climbed aboard, while Eric and Iris sat in the shade at one of the cleaner picnic tables.

"I'm not sure if she's told you, Iris, but I've asked your mom to legally adopt the boys."

Iris shook her head, "No, she didn't."

"When we talked about it, she thought it might also be a good idea for me to adopt you, too. And—," he held up his hand when he saw Iris's expression, "I would be happy to do that, but it's a very different situation. When their mother left us when they were just a year old, she gave up her rights to be their mom. But your dad didn't give you up and I don't want you to feel that I'm trying to replace him. It will only happen if *you* want it to, okay?"

Iris was looking towards the boys and trying not to cry. Eric leaned into her line of sight, waggling his eyebrows and waving around an imaginary cigar, "Those are my principles – and if you don't like those I have others."

She sniffed and gave him a wobbly smile. "Your Groucho Marx is improving."

"Thanks. Can I see your research? How did you and Ashley do your detective work?"

She told him about the Internet search and showed him the pictures, and Eric spent time reading through the pages while she pushed the boys on the swings. After hot dogs and sodas from a street corner stand for lunch, he and Iris played with the boys until they were worn out and ready for a nap.

Walking home, the twins were quiet for a change. It was an odd feeling, she thought, being so comfortable with Eric and dreading the next meeting with her mom.

But Jennifer wasn't home when they arrived. Eric put the boys down for a nap and Iris went to her room to do homework.

Instead, she lay on her bed looking at the pictures of her father, her grandparents and her uncle, wondering what it would be like to grow up on a Christmas tree farm.

At dinner that night, it was as though the morning's argument had never taken place. Iris wanted to bring up the subject again, but decided to wait like Eric suggested, to give her mom a chance to think about it.

When Eric and the boys left the kitchen, Jennifer asked Iris to stay. When she started to get up and clear the dishes, her mom stopped her.

"I'm sorry about this morning, Iris. It...your news took me by surprise."

"That's okay," Iris answered. When her mother didn't say anything further, she added, "Have you called them yet?"

Jennifer got up from the table, cleared a plate or two and then sat down again.

"Eric told me that he talked to you about the adoption plan this morning, and I think it's a good idea."

"Eric said he wouldn't if I didn't want him to, though."

"Iris, this is something that Eric and I discussed months ago, but the new baby and your discovery make it even more important to me. We... well, I, feel that it would be better to become one complete family and not look to the past."

"No!" Iris jumped to her feet, her chair slamming into the cupboard behind her. "Adopting me won't change who I am, and it won't change me wanting to know my grandparents!"

"Iris, sit down!"

"Why can't you understand –?"

"I *don't* understand. Why *is* this suddenly so important to you?"

"It's *always* been important, Mom! But you just never want to talk about it."

Her mom turned away for a moment and Iris was just about to run to her room when Jennifer answered. "You're right, I've never wanted to talk about my family, or what happened when you were born. I don't want to relive anything. I don't want to remember – for reasons you can't possibly understand."

"I can't understand if you won't tell me! And I don't want to be adopted. I want to meet my grandparents. The article said my grandfather's sick, sick enough to close their business! I *need* to meet him before it's too late!"

Even though the subject of her adoption wasn't brought up again, neither was the subject of her family tree or if she was going to be able to meet her grandparents anytime soon.

But it was hard to not think about since every time she worked on her homework, she saw their names and faces and the map to where they lived. The Google Earth picture looked down on the snow-covered rooftops and rows of trees and reminded her that they were real. She wished she had just called them like Ashley had suggested.

The homework assignment and display project were finished. After her mother's reaction, Iris hadn't even shown her the carefully drawn coat of arms, nor the artfully arranged albeit still stubby family tree. She knew no one would laugh and she knew she would get a good grade, but it wasn't complete.

Now that she knew her grandparents were out there, she felt restless and anxious and she couldn't seem to get them out of her mind, even though she wanted to.

Ten days until Christmas, life was just about back to normal and the school semester almost over when she found the papers. Searching for scissors and tape on her mom's desk to wrap a birthday present for Ashley, she found the letter from an attorney and legal paperwork for Eric to adopt her.

Weeks had passed since Charles's tumble, Thanksgiving had come and gone and now it was but ten days until Christmas. This year, Charles would be glad to see the other side of the holiday for very different reasons.

Time was slipping away into an indistinct haze of restless nights and lackluster days, with nothing much to break the routine except the abstract and very vivid dreams he had been plagued by lately. He used to sleep soundly and never remember his dreams, sometimes he was even a bit envious when Adele would recount a particularly funny or interesting dream.

This morning he lay still, remembering how he'd heard his grandfather's thundering voice from the trunk of a gnarly old oak tree, one knothole mouth uttering his usual invective and long, twisted limbs shaking with righteous indignation, all while he was incongruously planted in a field of flowers. A field of irises, Charles remembered, white, blue, purple, and yellow irises as far as the eye could see.

Apart from the nocturnal meandering of his

mind, there was an occasional visit from Jerry Lazarro or Brent Abbott, or the sudden gust of fresh air when Daniel, Sean and Hamid reported in regularly about their work out among the trees.

Great friends, even though they were so different. Quiet and serious Daniel, tall and lean, with dark hair and piercing gray eyes, Sean, burly and blond and always good for a laugh, and Hamid with his dark skin and his charming smile—or so said Adele one day, and Sean and Daniel had never let him live it down.

Damp from the rain and smelling of evergreens, sawdust, and sweat, they talked and laughed, downing glasses of milk or pots of coffee and consuming platefuls of Adele's scones or pumpkin spice cake in one sitting.

By God, he envied them and felt buoyed by their youth, strength, and vitality while they were in the room.

After they had left earlier, he had watched the bubbles on the side of Sean's milk glass slowly slide down and settle at the bottom, mirroring the sensation that overcame him in the now silent house. As though he were sliding slowly down, back into the torpor of uselessness that drained him, leaving him even weaker than before and deeply frustrated.

Bone-tired but restless. He had given up coffee completely believing caffeine was the cause of the jittery, fight-or-flight edginess, waking up with his jaw tightly clenched and legs tense and aching.

A nurturing and practical woman, he knew that

Adele was at a loss as to how to help him. In the weeks since the doctor had claimed he was showing signs of improving, Charles now used the wheelchair, grudgingly, for anything but the short walk from kitchen to bedroom.

She suggested it was time to get a second opinion. Far more than the disloyalty of mistrusting Alford, he hated the thought of another doctor poking and prodding at him and very likely foisting more pills on him.

Charles lay on the bed looking out at the gray skies and the water dripping from a crack in the gutter, unsure of the time. Adele had gone shopping, and he was relieved to have her out of the house. She didn't hover, she didn't mollycoddle, although he accused her of it often enough. Remembering the anxiety in her eyes as she left him this morning made his throat close with pain; her worry for him radiated through her with every look and gesture, only adding to the impotent fury he felt.

Useless.

Nearly dark when he opened his eyes, startled, almost as though someone had woken him urgently, he could have sworn he'd felt a hand on his shoulder. He sat up too quickly, only to be assailed with another of the overwhelming flushes of heat and dizziness that inevitably followed.

Before the spell had fully passed he opened his

bedside drawer, felt inside, and drew the rosary beads from their pouch. He sank awkwardly to the floor, his knees against the hard, cold wood, closed his eyes, and made the sign of the cross.

"I believe in God, the Father Almighty, Creator of heaven and earth...."

Chapter Nine

Three days after finding the adoption papers, and so early in the morning the sun hadn't even risen yet, Iris edged her way into the line of passengers boarding the bus, right behind a mom with three young children. That was Ashley's idea, a way to stay safe from strangers with evil intent, she had said with a meaningful look.

Iris waved once more to Ashley and then it was her turn to board. She beheld the three steep, metal steps and felt a sharp twist of fear in her stomach. Her hand shook as she reached for the handrail. But she had to get to her grandparents. Why she felt this so strongly when she had found out about them only a few weeks before she didn't know, but she *had* to go.

Her heart pounded, and her mouth was so dry it was good she didn't need to say anything to the bus driver. Ashley was worried the driver would question her about traveling alone, but the man was collecting tickets in one hand and texting on his phone with the other and didn't even glance up at the passengers as they boarded. Iris heard the old lady behind her say in a scolding tone of voice, "I do hope you'll look up from that thing when you're driving, young man!"

Iris took the empty seat next to the oldest of the three kids. Even before the rest of the passengers boarded, Iris was offering to read the books the girl pulled out of her backpack. Far from being upset, the mom, who was trying to settle both a crying baby and busy toddler, seemed thankful.

Between books, Iris glanced out the window at freeways, scrubby hillsides, grassy fields, barren fields, oil fields and sometimes an orange grove or some kind of orchard. Somewhere north of Bakersfield, she didn't need to see anything to know they had just passed a cattle ranch. After reading several books, some of them twice, little Suni fell asleep. Iris ate the lunch she had packed and looked out towards the far distant hills.

Iris had convinced her Mom to let her spend the first few days of the school holiday with Ashley, to escape the nightmare of going to Palm Springs to visit Eric's parents at their other house, a really nice house, but still. Ashley said that Jennifer probably felt guilty for not letting Iris call her grandparents, so she said yes to the normally outrageous request. Iris thought Eric might have helped convince her mom, too, and that made Iris feel even more guilty about what she was doing.

Ashley had done way more than give her an alibi. She helped get the tickets and even a ride to the station. One of Ashley's older cousins, Bianca, drove them, and another cousin, Madison, was a college student in the town of Sacramento, where Iris had to catch the little shuttle that went on to Placerville. Madison had promised to be waiting at the station when Iris arrived, and to alert Ashley if anything went wrong.

Iris woke up, startled, and dropped her own book she had been reading after Suni and family had disembarked in Manteca, surprised to hear the driver announce their arrival in Sacramento.

After gathering her things, she noticed the older woman and an elderly man one row up from her. During most of the trip the man had slept while the woman read a book, but now she was holding the man in a close but gentle embrace as he cried, his shoulders shaking as she patted his back. Iris felt a lump in her own throat and looked away, wondering why he cried.

Seeing other families on the bus made Iris think even more about her own. *Why* did her mother hate her own mother so much? Iris couldn't imagine anything keeping her from her mother, and grimaced, not even Mom's anger when she discovered what Iris had done.

She just hoped she could get home Monday without any fuss and then she would admit the truth and take the consequences.

What would it feel like, she wondered, when she was on the bus again, on her way home? What memories would she have in place of the anticipation she felt now?

Chapter Ten

WHAT HAVE I DONE?

Standing on the narrow country road, Iris watched the little bus slowly pull away.

A shiver, that had nothing to do with the chilly December night, started at the back of her neck and traveled all the way down her spine. She wished she had answered differently when the driver had asked, "Sure this is the right stop, miss?"

Now, the cheerful holiday music slowly faded away, and the tail lights shrank to tiny ruby dots in the twilight before the bus finally disappeared around a bend in the road.

She turned and walked towards the nearest driveway.

"Hello. My name is Iris Gibson and I'm..." her voice sounded loud and unnatural in the cold night air. She cleared her throat and continued, practicing aloud what she had in her imagination on the long bus ride north. "Hi, my name is Iris and your son Andrew was my father..." now hearing a tremble, she cleared her throat again. "Hello, my name is Iris and I'm your granddaughter... Hi, my name is Iris and I'm, ah, I'm—ouch!" she cried, tripping on a rock in the road. "An *idiot!*"

She threw off her backpack and dropped down on the bank next to the big sign, painted a glossy, dark green with large gold letters, which heralded the entrance to her grandparents' farm, grateful for the tiny lantern that hung above, and the reassuring patch of light in the deepening darkness. A small 'Closed for the Season' sign hung over the larger one, squeaking softly as it swayed back and forth in the breeze.

A screech suddenly pierced the silence.

Iris jumped up, ready to run but by the time she reached for her backpack, she remembered the owl expert who had come to school. *An owl,* she thought, trying to calm her racing heart, just one of those creepy white-faced barn owls. Farther in the distance she heard a different call, and even though the resonant, haunting query of the great-horned owl was not as startling, it sent another shiver rushing down her back.

She sat back down, near the old gray mailbox with her own last name so prominently displayed in fading black letters. Only three days ago with Ashley, the plan made so much sense and seemed like it would be so easy. Now it was just...unreal.

Dried leaves crackled beneath her as she lay back and looked up at the sky.

"What have I done?" she whispered, shivering again from fear and the cold that already numbered her toes and penetrated the thin fabric of her jacket.

The horizon was still as pale as a robin's egg, but high above stars were shining in the darkening blue.

"Starlight, star bright, first star I see tonight..." searching the stars overhead, she paused, wondering what exactly she should wish for "...I wish I may, I wish I might, have the wish I wish tonight."

Now, eleven hours and two buses from L.A. and here she was, at the entrance to her grandparents' farm searching the sky and wishing she was home. But nothing had happened, no shooting stars or comets marking her wish across the universe and transporting her home, only a satellite and Iris didn't think they counted for wishes. The breeze grew stronger and the night darker.

The air was different here, Iris thought, breathing in deeply of some tangy, rich aroma, feeling a cool dampness in her lungs. She had brought her warmest jacket and some gloves, but her nose was already cold and she could feel a chill from the ground right through her coat. She sat up and pulled the strap of her backpack over her arm just as several street lights along the farm driveway lit up.

The revving of an engine, a loud engine, from the same direction broke the silence. Iris crawled farther up the bank and hid behind the sign, watching as a battered old pick-up truck rattled down the drive and out onto the road. Taking the turn too fast, its backend fishtailed and Iris ducked her head back just before loose gravel sprayed up the bank and against the thick wood of the sign.

She stayed still until the sound of the engine faded in the distance, and then pulled out her phone and called Ashley.

"I'm here."

"Hi! Have you met your grandparent's yet? What's the farm like?"

"I haven't even walked up the road yet! I'm scared, Ash. Somebody just drove out of here *really* fast, like there's something wrong in there. I don't know what to do!"

"Maybe you could call them and talk with them first, before you go up to the house—"

"What if they say 'no, go away!'? I'm miles away from anything else. I'm cold and hungry, and I have to pee really bad!"

Ashley laughed. "Geez, Iris, you're like three of the 101 Dalmatians!"

"Ha, ha! You can laugh! Just tell me what to do!"

"We went over this, remember, you were just going to walk up and knock on the door?"

"I know, but it was different when I was there. Now I'm scared."

"How about if you go up and say you're lost? Then you can meet them before you have to tell them who you are. Or, I could call them and tell them you're out there, do you want me to?" Iris thought about what to do as Ashley rattled off half a dozen different ways to get into the farmhouse without actually walking right up, knocking on the door and admitting the truth.

"Shh!" Iris whispered when she heard footsteps approaching her hiding place. A woman's voice was quietly scolding someone. Iris peered out from around the sign again.

Adele Gibson appeared older than her website photos, but Iris would have known her even if she hadn't seen the Gibson plaid scarf draped over the collar of her brown corduroy jacket. A small and rather shaggy dog ran at her side, but then stopped and sniffed the air once it got to the end of the driveway.

Iris drew back behind the sign, still gripping her phone to her ear, hearing the panic in Ashley's voice, "What's going on? *Iris*?" Iris held her breath and nearly choked when her grandmother called out:

"All right, young lady, are you still out here? If you are, come out right now! The bus driver called and told me you got off here, so come out where I can see you!"

The dog was already sniffing around the sign and whimpering excitedly, so Iris knew she had no choice. "It's okay, but I'd better go," she whispered to Ashley. "I'll call you later."

She snapped her phone shut and shoved it into her pocket, just as the dog started to bark. She stepped out from behind the sign and jumped down the small embankment to the driveway, feeling Adele Gibson's sharp gaze on her with every step. When she looked up, she met her grandmother's eyes.

In the light of the street lamps, Iris could see strands of silver glinting in her grandmother's short red hair. Her dramatically arched eyebrows gave Adele Gibson a very stern appearance, but as she looked Iris up and down, Iris could see her grandmother's expression soften as her gaze lingered momentarily on Iris's hair.

The dog was barking, whining and jumping on her.

"Hush, Darby!" Her grandmother snapped her fingers and he sat, but kept whimpering and wagging his tail so hard his whole body trembled.

"I'm glad to see that you're all right after that hooligan sped out of here. What is your excuse for coming here uninvited like this?" her grandmother said, the frown returning. "Well?" she prompted when Iris didn't, couldn't, answer.

"I...I..." All of the lame introductions she'd had running through her head were gone. How could it be that her grandmother already knew about her?

Her grandmother crossed her arms and continued to look stern. "Of all the crazy kids who have ever pulled this stunt, you have got to be the youngest. Just how old are you?"

"Tw...twelve," Iris managed to stammer, "Ma'am" she added, seeing the eyebrows arch even higher. Who were all these crazy kids she was talking about?

"You seem...familiar," again the expression in her eyes softened as she looked closely at Iris's face. "Were you with one of the Placerville groups this summer?"

Iris could only shake her head, relieved her grandmother didn't know who she was but dreading the moment to come.

"No?" Her grandmother searched Iris's face again. "Well, never mind then. Come on back to the house and we'll call your folks."

Perceptive to his mistress's change of tone, the dog ran to Iris once again whimpering and wagging his tail in a frenzy of welcome.

"Darby! Home!" her grandmother said sharply, clapping her hands, sending him running back up the driveway. And then, with a hint of a smile, she stepped closer to Iris and held out her hand.

"My name is Adele Gibson and you don't have to be frightened. I'm told *my* bark is worse than my bite. What is your name?"

Iris hesitated for just a moment and then took her grandmother's hand. Even though their first touch was through her glove, she felt as though she was going to cry and didn't let go as her grandmother began to draw back her hand. She took a deep breath and said, "My name is Iris Christine Gibson, and I'm...I'm your granddaughter."

Iris could see the color drain from her grandmother's face. She wasn't sure if it was sadness or something else in her eyes as she once again looked at Iris, at her eyes, mouth, and lingering longest on her hair. Iris was beginning to worry and kicking herself for not lying when her grandmother, her voice almost a whisper, said, "I don't understand...*Iris*?"

"Andrew was my father...Andrew Stewart Gibson, who was born on October twenty-second..." She stammered out the details she remembered from his birth certificate, relieved to see color beginning to return to her grandmother's face. "I'm sorry, Mrs. Gibson. I didn't want to upset you. That's why I was hiding. Once I got here, I didn't know how to tell you, and, well... I was...scared."

Once she could speak again, her grandmother's voice shook. "Well... I don't know what to say, except that I do believe you, my dear, of course I do, and I'm so... so very happy you're here."

Iris didn't know what else to say either as her grandmother began to cry but was relieved when her grandmother's arms finally closed around her. She hugged back and just waited.

When her grandmother drew away, she pulled a tissue from her jacket pocket and wiped her eyes. "There's no doubt at all that you're my grandchild. I should have known immediately...," she said, giving Iris a shaky smile, reaching out and gently touching her hair. "Now, why don't we walk up to the house and you can explain exactly how it is that you have materialized here on this particular night."

Walking slowly up the long driveway, Iris told her everything. Her grandmother listened intently, nodding in understanding, giving a little laugh a time or two. When they reached the farmhouse, she sat down on a wooden bench near the door and patted the seat beside her.

"That is quite a tale, Iris Christine Gibson and you have certainly changed since the first time we met."

They sat quietly for a while and Iris looked around at the barn and other buildings, trees, shrubs and other things she could see in the light of the lamps. The owls screeched and hooted in the distance and she could feel the vibration of her cell phone in her coat pocket. Ashley must be going crazy, she thought.

"Your mother was quite ill, from grief and a difficult birth, and I've never been quite sure if she even remembered we were there. Her good friends were staying with you, caring for the two of you, so Charles, Alexander and I came back home a few days after Andrew's funeral. We offered to help in any way we could, and invited you both to come and stay whenever she might want, but we never did hear from her. We tried to contact her through the school, but we were never able to find where you had moved."

"She never wrote or anything…?"

"Please don't judge your mother harshly, Iris," her grandmother said quickly, reaching over to brush the hair away from her eyes. "We don't know what happened once she left the hospital. Her grief and recovery, and caring for a new baby, might have been all she could manage. Remember," she added, "your mother was very young, only nineteen years old, poor thing. But you have both always been in our prayers."

They sat together quietly for another moment.

"Who was in the truck that drove out so fast?"

Iris asked.

"Truck?" said her grandmother, as though she had forgotten all about it. "Oh, that was a young friend, Daniel, who wanted to talk with your grandfather and I wouldn't let him tonight. It was very unlike him to behave that way and nothing to worry about."

"Um… who did you think I was when you saw me?" Iris asked.

Her grandmother laughed. "Ah, that must have sounded quite harsh, but you see, over the years we have had summer helpers that come from one of the local youth camps. Many come from very difficult homes. Occasionally, one will think of us when they want to run away, and usually that's in the midst of our busy season. I suppose they think they can blend in here and work away like little elves. It's sad, really; they are just running to a place where they've had a happy memory."

"Have you ever kept one before?" Iris asked, shivering.

"Just long enough to scold over a cup of hot cocoa and call their parents." Her grandmother paused, looking closely at Iris. "I cannot begin to tell you how truly happy I am that you are here, Iris, but before we go in and warm up, there are two things I have to tell you. I know you will understand the first and you *must* obey the second.

"As you read in your thorough research, your grandfather Charles has been rather ill lately. When we go inside I will go and talk with him quietly for a few moments. We can't go giving him any sudden shocks. Do you understand?"

Iris nodded and waited.

"You must call your mother and tell her you are here, even if she does believe you are safely with a friend for the weekend," she smiled at Iris's expression. "I know you're upset with her for not allowing you to contact us, but she loves you and was only worried about you. She must know where you are, truthfully. Will you do that?"

Iris nodded again, but felt even more fear than when the bus had pulled away.

Her grandmother seemed to understand and held out her hand to Iris, "You were a brave girl to travel all the way to see us, a *bad* girl, mind you, but brave. You just have to be brave one more time tonight."

Chapter Eleven

CHARLES HEARD ADELE OPEN the bedroom door and step inside quietly. He began to turn but heard her draw a deep, unsteady breath, and waited a moment longer to fully open his eyes and turn to her as she wiped away tears and took a deep breath to steady herself.

"Was that Daniel a while ago?" he asked, pretending not to notice. "Surely there's no other truck as loud as his."

"He wanted to talk with you – he seemed quite upset about something. I didn't want him to...to trouble you tonight."

His eyes still half closed, Charles said wearily. "I'll call him in the morning."

Adele turned her face away to wipe away more tears.

"What is it, *mo chridhe?*" he asked gently, as she sat beside him.

"I have something to tell you, Charles."

"Aye?"

"Pete Henderson called earlier, to tell me we had another summer camper come to call. Of course, that was right when Daniel was here, so it took me a few minutes to walk out to the road…"

Charles shifted his position and slowly sat up.

"Adele, it isna like you to babble. Which one is it? That little tow-headed mite that followed you around like a puppy?"

Adele's expression lightened and she smiled at the memory. "Zach? You know, that's who crossed my mind when Pete called…" She paused, gripping his hand firmly. "But no, Charles, this is a girl. A beautiful, redheaded, twelve-year-old, girl."

Tears began to fall again as she saw realization begin to dawn in Charles's eyes. "She was hiding behind the sign, and I yelled at her! She hopped down, stood in front of me stammering and was so scared. Something was so familiar about her, but I was just blind!"

She gave a long shuddering sob as Charles took her in his arms. "It's Iris, Charles! Iris is here."

When the bedroom door closed behind her grandmother, Iris made a beeline for the bathroom and then sent Ashley a text to tell her she'd met her grandmother and everything was okay. She didn't stop to read the ten messages Ashley had frantically sent while waiting, but walked slowly around the living room as she sipped her hot cocoa. Even though she was still nervous about meeting her grandfather, and especially about calling her mother, the panic was gone. She had met her grandmother, the house was warm and welcoming and even smelled good, like vanilla from the big white candle burning on the deep living room windowsill.

Paintings of the farmhouse and trees, and photographs of different people and places hung on the walls. Books, plants and delicate, pretty things adorned the shelves and window sills, and on the top of the piano were several pictures of her father and uncle, as babies, little boys and young men. Evergreen trees were almost always in the pictures as the boys planted or cut or hauled trees. In one of them, the boys fought a pretend duel, holding two long pine branches as their swords.

One stood out from the others. She picked up a small white frame adorned with pink rosebuds with a photograph of a boy about her age sitting with a very little baby in a rocking chair, a nurse standing near. She gasped and felt another shiver go through her as she read the faded writing along the lower edge of the photo, *Alexander and Iris*.

Uncle Alexander, holding me! She looked more closely, at his blue and white striped shirt, and his tousled red hair that was just like the bit of hers showing above the pink, white and blue blanket. Alexander had a short, rather snub nose and a face covered with freckles, and in every other picture on the piano he smiled or made funny faces, but holding her, his expression was sad. A nurse stood in the background, her hand resting on the clear bassinet with a little, beaded bracelet and an "I'm a Girl!" card.

She set it down carefully and stepped into a dark alcove of the living room and flipped a switch.

"Wow," Iris's eyes traveled over all the beautiful things that were suddenly illuminated by strings of small golden lights along each of the glass shelves.

Christmas ornaments, each one on its own gold or silver stand, were displayed on shelves painted a deep, glossy green. Each stand was labeled with a date, and Iris recognized the first one because it was the same rich red ball with the band of Gibson tartan that she and Ashley had seen on the website. The most recent was soft grayish blue with snow-covered trees.

Iris searched for the year she was born and found it easily because it was very different from the rest. A pure white ball encircled with a band of golden fleurs-de-lis and evergreen boughs tied with ribbons of Gibson tartan. *Wow*, she thought, pulling out her phone and taking a picture, *wait till I show Ashley!*

Other cabinets in the alcove held beautiful Christmas books, teacups and saucers, painted tins with holiday scenes, mostly Christmas trees. She switched off the light and went back out into the living room where the wood-paneled walls gleamed in the soft lamplight, reminding her of the dark honey her mom liked in her tea. The kitchen and dining room were open to the living room and dark green curtains framed all the windows.

She rinsed her cup and set it in the sink and looked out the window, finding it strange that curtains weren't closed tight against the darkness as they always were at home in their apartment.

White shelves in the kitchen displayed pretty, painted tea cups and mugs, pie plates, gravy boats and things, and there were scrolls, flowers and fleurs-de-lis in the raised pattern of the shiny silver walls behind the sink and under some of the cabinets.

Even after the cocoa, her stomach rumbled from sniffing the aroma wafting from the big, black pot simmering on the stove. Back in the living room, she sat down to wait on the big, soft couch.

A cup and saucer decorated with deep red and golden yellow roses sat on a nearby table, as well as a big, hardcover book and a pair of glasses. Her grandmother must have been sitting here when the person in the truck arrived and the bus driver called. She listened for the sound of her grandparents' voices but couldn't hear anything other than the soft music from the radio.

The sofa was soft and comfortable, warm air began wafting over her from a vent nearby, the music was as pretty as a lullaby and Iris could feel her eyes growing heavy.

I'll just close my eyes for a minute...just for a minute.

Chapter Twelve

THE AROMA OF WHATEVER she had seen simmering on the stove was the first thing she noticed when she woke. Woke, but couldn't quite open her eyes, but she did notice something warm next to her. She reached out; Darby the dog was curled up next to her, his chin resting on her knee.

She rubbed her eyes and yawned.

"Hello there, wee Gibson. Looks as though you've made a friend."

Her gray-haired grandfather, wrapped up in a thick bathrobe, was sitting in a wheelchair near the sofa, looking at her with a slight smile on his lips and a twinkle in his blue eyes. The sound of her grandmother's humming came from the kitchen.

"Hello," she said. "Is that a Scottish accent?"

"Aye, lassie, that it is," he answered, "but I'll have you know it's called a br-rogue and not an accent, like I'm some kind of a Sassenach!"

"Oh, okay," she said, as she sat up and stretched.

Maybe Ashley was right, she thought, maybe her grandfather was a mean old grump. "What's a sassynack?"

"A Sassenach is someone not from Scotland. An outlander, aye?"

"Oh...am I an outlander?" she asked.

"Ach no, lass. You're a Gibson and we'll have you rolling your r's in no time," he said, now smiling at Adele when she sat on the sofa next to Iris.

"I'm glad you had a bit of a nap, Iris. Did you call your mother?"

Iris shook her head. "No... I thought I would wait till you were here, in case she wanted... well, I *know* she'll want to talk to you." Iris pulled her cell phone out of her pocket and asked hopefully, "Do you want to call her?"

Her grandmother smiled but shook her head.

"No, my dear. The voice she needs to hear first is your own. Be sure you start out with the fact that you're all right, though, you don't want her to worry too much. Tell her you are sorry, too, that may help a little."

"There's no use in trying to soften things up for the little vagrant. You know the lass will be getting a fair helping of tongue pie."

"Charles!" she scolded, adjusting the blanket over him. "I'll thank you not to call our granddaughter a vagrant!"

Iris was wondering what exactly a vagrant was, and hoping it wasn't tongue pie that she smelled cooking in the kitchen as she listened to the ring, but forgot everything else when she heard her mother's voice. Only silence answered her after she told her mom what she had done. In the long pause, Iris reassured her that she was fine, that she was safe and that she was really, *really* sorry.

And then the pause was over.

"My God, Iris," her mother said in a breathless sort of voice, reminding Iris of her own the time she'd gotten the wind knocked out of her.

"Mom…?"

"My God, Iris, how *could* you?" she whispered in the same hard to breathe kind of way. Iris wished she would just go ahead and yell.

"Mom….?"

Her mother didn't answer, but Iris could hear talking in the background.

"Iris? Are you okay?" Eric came on the phone, his usually mellow voice sharp with worry. "What's happened?"

Another long pause after she repeated what she had said to her mother.

"Wow," he said, and she could tell he had relaxed, as soon as he found out she was safe. "I can't believe you did this, Iris."

"Well," she almost whispered. "I felt like I had to. Once I knew they were here, I couldn't get it out of my head."

She felt uncomfortable trying to explain with her grandparents near. Noticing this, her grandmother went into the kitchen and her grandfather made an exaggerated show of looking around the room. Darby, however, was still beside her, cocking his head from side to side, his deep brown gaze fixed intently on the phone.

"I was afraid …well …"

"Afraid?"

"Well, I was afraid that if you adopted me that Mom would never let me—"

"Iris, I know we're still getting to know each other, but you *can* trust my promise not to adopt you if it's not what you want. And, you may not agree with her decisions, but you must know your mother only wants the best for you. *And* you might have considered disobeying with a letter, or a telephone call. Don't you realize how incredibly dangerous this was, for you to take off on your own?"

She'd never heard Eric sound so serious or angry and he had never scolded her before. Iris suddenly realized what her grandfather had meant by 'a fair helping of tongue pie.'

"I'm sorry."

He sighed, and Iris could almost see him pinching that spot between his eyes, the way he did when the boys did something *really* annoying. "I know you are, but the most important thing right now is that you're safe. Are you *sure* you're all right? You honestly feel *completely* safe there for tonight?"

"Yes, I really do—*really*," Iris said in a rush, "and I have my ticket home for Monday. It's not like I ran away…forever…or anything," she added, trying to keep herself from laughing when she saw her grandfather start to chuckle and heard her grandmother trying to shush him.

"Well then," she could hear the smile in his voice again, as though he could hear them in the background. "Better let me talk to one of your grandparents, Iris."

Iris handed the phone to her grandmother, who took it with a wink and walked into the kitchen. Iris and Charles listened to the one-sided conversation. "Absolutely no need to apologize" and "I can't begin to tell you how very pleased we are to have her here." and "We will simply accept this unexpected blessing and, truly, she couldn't have arrived at a better time."

Iris was beginning to breathe easier when she heard her grandmother make a startling suggestion.

"Why don't you call our local sheriff, Brent Abbott?"

Charles chuckled again at her expression. "Now you've done it, wee Gibson."

"Yes, talk with him. Explain what has happened and that Iris is with us. He's a longtime family friend and I'm sure it would help you both feel better. Let me give you his number and ours, and you can phone us right back."

The seconds seem to crawl by while they waited for the phone to ring. Charles tried to keep Iris preoccupied by asking about her class project that brought her to them. As she pulled the research from her backpack to show him, the telephone rang.

Her grandmother answered in the kitchen and there was a brief pause before she said in a shaking voice, "Jennifer approves of her staying? Wonderful! Thank you so much, Eric. Please tell her she must call anytime, and that we'll take great care of Iris."

Iris sighed in relief.

"You must lead a charmed life, wee Gibson," her grandfather said, smiling and shaking his head. "Now, wheel me over to the kitchen so we can bang our cups on the table and demand our supper. Otherwise, we'll be wasting away and waiting all night for your grandmother to stop her fussing over you."

A short time later, her grandmother placed the large steaming pan in front of them. Iris had never eaten lamb stew before, not that her mother had told her about anyway. But she was so hungry and the browned meat, potatoes and green beans simmering in thick, golden gravy smelled so delicious, she accepted the first helping without hesitation.

"You know, Adele, there's only one way to know if the girl is a *real* member of the family," her grandfather said in a stern voice. His smile was gone, but a twinkle still glinted in his eyes.

"That's true, dear," her grandmother nodded, ladling a serving onto his plate, "but if you don't mind, let's not test her at our very first meal together."

"I think if she's found us and come all this way, she'll not be opposed to answering one simple thing." He turned to her. "Now would you?"

Iris shook her head and glanced back and forth

at them, starting to feel nervous again and wondering what kind of test they were talking about. She reached for the pepper and applied it liberally over her dinner before remembering her mother's admonition about being polite and tasting her food first.

Wondering why her grandfather hadn't asked his question, she looked up, pepper shaker still in her hand. Her grandparents were both looking at her and she was surprised to see tears glistening in her grandmother's eyes and a grin slowly spreading across her grandfather's face.

He raised his glass to her, "Welcome to the family, Iris Christine Gibson. Now pass the pepper."

"These are obviously good people, Jen," said Eric, his hand stroking Jennifer's back as she cried against his shoulder. "After talking with Sheriff Abbott, I'd even leave the boys with them."

From the other room, the sound of the twins arguing loudly over something reached them and he added with a hopeful expression. "Could we take them now?"

She raised her head and gave him a teary smile and wiped her eyes. "How did she find them? How did she even get their names in the first place? I've never told her!"

"She's been working on her family tree for three months! They would be on the certificates she used for her project."

"But I only meant to give her mine and hers!"

Eric's look of confusion was quickly replaced by guilt. "I saw the envelope next to the one you asked me to set out for her, and I thought they were supposed to be together...

"*You* gave them to her?"

"I thought that was the whole idea, sweetheart, to give her something for her family tree."

"Maybe that's just your way of saying you don't really want to adopt her!" She stood up. "Is that it? I thought you were just trying to ease her into the idea, but ..."

"Jen," he said, gently, taking her hand. "I would adopt Iris in a heartbeat. I *do* love Iris like she's my own—she's a wonderful person and a huge credit to you. But this is between me and Iris and I won't push adoption, not if she doesn't want it."

She sank back onto the chair, covering her face with her hands.

"I'm sorry I misunderstood about the certificates. It honestly never occurred to me you wouldn't want her to have all of them." He stood up and poured tea for both of them.

"But I'm not sorry it happened. No, not Iris taking a bus alone for three hundred miles," he amended quickly, "but she needed to meet her grandparents. She's safe and in good hands and you are not going to lose her to them. For one thing, she loves you very much and the two of you have a great relationship. They're no threat to you."

Iris had thought that sitting down to dinner together for the first time would be strange, but it wasn't. They asked her questions about school, about where she had grown up, and more about her class project. She asked questions about the farm, and her grandfather told her he would take her on a tour the next day, even though her grandmother said, "Now Charles…"

"I'm going to ride around on a little cart, Adele, how taxing can that be? I *can* still walk. That idiot doctor only confined me to this damned contraption to, what did he say, 'preserve my strength'? Draining what strength I have left, is more like it, just like those bloody pills of his."

Her grandmother had her arms crossed and was looking at him with that arched eyebrow of hers, sort of like she was saying something to him with just her eyes.

"The lass can use her wee phone and call out the National Guard if we get into trouble. What do you say to that?"

"One hour, that's what I have to say," her grandmother answered, trying to look stern, but Iris could tell she liked the idea of her grandfather showing her the farm.

After dinner, when her grandmother suggested

it was time to let Iris settle in and for Charles to get some rest, Charles paused on the way to the bedroom, taking Iris's hands in his.

"You're not going to disappear before morning, are you, wee Gibson, like some kind of Sídhe?"

"A shay? What's that?"

"Fairy."

"Oh." Iris smiled and shook her head. "No, because if it's still all right with Grandmother, you're going to take me on a tour of the farm tomorrow."

Charles chuckled. "So, you've already figured out who's in charge around here."

"That's enough of that, you two," her grandmother said, making a tsking sound at both of them as Charles winked at her and went off to the bedroom. "Come along, Iris, let's get you settled in."

The stairwell was narrow, lit with just a bare bulb sticking out of the wall and wooden stairs, each step creaking underfoot.

"The light will stay on all night. I don't like the idea of dark stairways, especially for you, not being used to the place yet.

"Since Alexander went away to school, I don't come up here very often. It will be good for these old rooms to feel like part of the house again." Grandmother opened the second door from the stairs and flipped a switch that illuminated a bedroom.

"This was your father's bedroom, Iris. Would you like it to be yours when you visit?"

Iris nodded while looking at several pictures of

her father on the wall.

"I'm glad. Now, why don't you tuck your clothes in the top drawer of the dresser while I tidy up."

Iris set down her backpack and put away the few things she had brought. Her grandmother made up the bed with fresh sheets and blankets.

"We never meant for this room to become a shrine, Iris, as some people might call leaving your father's things out like this. But we found that some of the pictures and things were too precious to pack away completely." She finished by straightening a thick floral comforter over the bed. "But now that you're here, I'm very glad there are still some mementos and personal things for you to see. It will help you to know more about him."

Iris could tell that her grandmother was trying not to cry; she had that shaky sound in her voice again.

"Now, is there anything you need, Iris? No? The bathroom is just next door, and if you need anything at all, anytime, you just come downstairs and tap on our bedroom door. If you wake up hungry and want a snack, help yourself to milk in the fridge, cookies in the cookie jar or scones in the bowl with the big, blue flowers. There's always a night light or two, so the house is never completely dark."

Iris nodded, suddenly feeling a little nervous about being upstairs all alone for the night.

"I know you're used to living in a big city, but this is a very safe place, Iris." How did her grandmother seem to know what she was thinking? "You will hear some noises in the night, that's for sure. On the inside, it's usually the old furnace, or the walls creaking because of the wind or cold. On the outside, there are the owls hooting and screeching, and tree branches that rustle and scratch against the house. There's nothing at all to worry about. All right?"

Iris nodded, and her grandmother reached out to touch her lightly on the shoulder.

"Good night, my dear."

Iris was still for a moment after her grandmother left, gazing at the grouping of photographs on the wall, several of her father as a baby, toddler and little boy surrounding a large one in the center. In that picture, he was a young man, looking straight into the camera and smiling broadly, almost as though he was about to laugh. Who had he been looking at? What had made him so happy?

After getting ready for bed, she called her mother to say goodnight, and that she was sorry, again. *About a hundred times*, Iris thought, but was relieved that her mom sounded more herself and didn't seem angry at her anymore, just worried.

On the bookshelf were pictures, baseball trophies, some old books and school yearbooks. In one of the desk drawers were a bundle of letters, a small Bible and a necklace with light blue beads with a silver cross. She didn't pull the books off the shelf. She didn't read any of the letters. She just looked at everything and reminded herself that she would be able to learn something new about her father every day.

Tonight, her brain was so full that her head almost hurt, but in the good way that a full stomach did after a really good dinner. She crawled into bed and shut off the light. She didn't expect to sleep with the memories of the day running through her mind.

She heard the owl again, but this time the low, echoing call didn't frighten her. Was it only a few hours ago that she was staring up at the sky and wishing on the stars that she had never come?

She wasn't sure what had woken her. The room was cool, but the comforter was thick and warm. She lay there in the shadows, thinking about her father in the bedroom where he had slept almost every night of his life.

Through a crack in the curtains, she saw a light that she hadn't noticed when she first went to bed. She got up and pulled the curtains back, gasping at the view spread out before her.

When Iris had been sitting in front of Ashley's computer screen and learned that her grandparents owned a Christmas tree farm, she envisioned something like the tree lot where she and her mom used to go buy their trees each December, even after seeing pictures on the website. But, the light from a very full moon illuminated rows and rows of dark evergreens that reached and spread over the rolling hills. The moonlight was so bright she could make out

distinct shapes of different kinds of trees. She couldn't
see another light anywhere, just the moon, stars, and
trees.

Everything was so different here, she thought,
climbing back into the warm bed, remembering the
ocean of concrete that spread out around her on the bus
ride out of Los Angeles, and the miles of boring fields
and rocky, grass-covered hills along the road north.

How could the moon be bigger here than at
home, she wondered? The light was so bright it almost
hurt her eyes, but she was spellbound by all the
shadows and patterns in its man-in-the-moon face. Iris
stared at it until her eyes finally closed and she slept

Chapter Thirteen

DARBY WAS CURLED UP at her feet, and daylight and the aroma of bacon filled the room the next time Iris woke. As soon as she moved, he wiggled his way up the bed for attention and she was petting him when her phone buzzed.

"Hey, Mom!"

"Hi, honey. Did I wake you?"

"Nope, I just woke up a minute ag--," she said, interrupted by a yawn and a stretch that accidentally pushed Darby off the bed.

"I thought I would call and say good morning and see how you're doing before it got too noisy around here. Any plans for the day?"

"After breakfast, Grandpa is going to take me on a tour of the farm on some kind of a cart. After that, I'm not sure."

"So Mr. Gibson must be feeling better. That's good."

"Well," Iris said, laughing, "Grandmother is letting us go out for an hour. Then he has to come back to rest."

"Grandmother, but Grandpa – not Grandfather?"

"No," Iris paused, smiling. "Grandmother. Grandpa. It just suits, I guess."

"What's for breakfast?"

Iris sniffed, "I know there's bacon, and it's making my stomach growl!"

"Well then, you'd better not keep them waiting. Give me a call later?"

Sunlight was streaming into the windows, and, unlike at home, there was no effort to draw blinds and shut out light or heat. Her grandmother sat with her back in the full sun, sipping something hot from a delicate teacup patterned with sprigs of green holly with bright red berries.

Iris felt self-conscious and paused before walking into the kitchen. They both looked up from what they were reading and smiled at her as she stepped around the corner.

Her grandfather, winking at her, reached over and pulled out the chair next to him.

"Good morning, Iris. Did you sleep well?" her grandmother asked, taking off her glasses.

She told them about waking up to the moonlight. "I could see the hills and all the trees, almost like the sun was shining. Is the moon bigger here or something?" she asked, before sipping the cocoa her grandmother had just set before her.

"Away from the lights and smog of the big city, the moon is bound to seem bigger and brighter to you," said Grandpa.

When her grandmother cleared and set the table to serve breakfast, she noticed they had been reading her research.

"These are most illuminating as well, wee Gibson," her grandfather said. "When did you get this particular article?"

"The day after Thanksgiving. See," she pointed to the date printed on the page. "But I think it was written a long time ago. Ashley said it was old news."

"Old news, indeed," he said, in a grumbly voice that matched his expression, at least until he set the papers aside and looked at Iris again.

"Daniel was upset about something last night," Adele said, putting a platter full of bacon, scrambled eggs, and fried potatoes on the table. "It must be about all of this. I'll give Jerry a call later and ask him what happened at the last meeting. Now, eat up, you two. This will help keep you warm while you're out among the trees."

After the sunlit warmth of the kitchen, Iris was surprised by how cold it was outside and glad to have her grandmother's hat and scarf. A light frost covered the ground, fence rails and shrubs in the shadows of the house.

Charles grumbled, but used his wheelchair to

get to a small shed nearest the house where he started up a little tractor. Almost like a golf cart, she thought, but this cart had a small pickup bed in the back that carried tools and buckets and a big bundle of coarse brown cloth.

After bypassing the huge gray barn, he turned uphill. When they reached the fence line at the high end of one row, he turned onto a new trail and stopped the cart. Behind them, a hill and a large grove of tall trees blocked the sun.

He seemed to be waiting for something. She looked up at him, but he just gestured towards the long trail that sloped below them.

"These are the Ponderosa pines, lass, see how they have longer needles than the rest? Wait and watch, just another minute or two."

Iris was glad to feel the warmth of the sun hit her back and then her grandfather said, "Now, wee Gibson, watch the line between sun and shadow."

Watching so hard her eyes watered, it was like a huge curtain, she thought, being very slowly drawn aside, and then the shadows were gone. Her grandfather drove down the row, droplets on the tips of the bright green needles sparkled in the bright sunlight and sprinkled them as the cart brushed against the branches on its way down the hill.

When they reached the bottom, laughing and wiping the water off their faces, he slowed and turned the cart down another row of trees, and then another. He pointed out the different kinds of trees, like the

Noble Fir, Blue Spruce, and Scots Pine, and even a tract of the biggest trees, the Giant Sequoia. He showed her the different cones and seeds and explained a bit about the stages of growth and when they planted and transplanted, pruned and sold. Some trees were sold for landscaping, he explained, but most of their business was during the Christmas season.

When their hour was nearly gone, Iris saw that her grandmother had been right. Being up and around had tired her grandfather.

"Is our hour almost up, Grandpa?"

Even though he grumbled something about not needing mollycoddling at his age, he turned the cart towards the farmhouse.

All along the different tracts, he talked to the trees and would stop and reach out to touch the boughs to feel the softness of the needles, more like they were animals that needed tending to, the way a cow needed to be milked or a dog needed to be petted, Iris thought. He even said a few things she didn't understand and he caught her watching him quizzically.

"The Gaelic," he explained, "seems to me a better language to talk to the trees."

"Oh," she said, not sure what to say about that.

"Don't worry, lass, they very seldom answer back." He winked, and put the cart into gear but stopped again soon at an area with several varieties of seedlings.

"Pick your favorite, wee Gibson," he said, reaching back into the pickup bed for something and handing it to her.

She looked at him, looked at the pitchfork and then back to him.

"Go on then. I'll tell you what to do."

She had been surprised by how many different types of trees there were along the rows, but she put her hand on one that reminded her of the Christmas tree she and her mother always picked and looked back at her grandfather.

"That's a nice little Blue Spruce. All right then, put the fork on the ground about two feet out...that's right. Now jump on it. Just like you're jumping on a pogo stick."

Pogo stick? What's that, she wondered, but knew what he meant anyway and jumped up, landed on the fork, teetered for a moment and then fell back onto her butt. Her grandfather grinned down at her.

"Keep at it, lass, you'll get the hang of it," he said, reaching out from the cart to help her up.

She found a softer spot in the soil, jumped hard and the prongs sank deep into the earth. He told her how to loosen the soil all around and then in one final jump and push, the little tree lifted out of the ground.

He handed her a big piece of the rough cloth, a burlap sack, he called it, and explained how to gently lift the tree with its root ball to the sack and then lift it into the back of the cart. Just when her arms were filled with the heavy mound of dirt, the prickly ends of the spruce boughs getting caught in her hair and poking her nose, she felt the vibration of her cell phone in her pocket. Mom won't believe this, she thought, hoping the story would be a good excuse for not answering her phone.

"What are we going to do with it?" she asked, as she climbed into the cart and he started back to the barn.

"Plant it. Later on today, at sunset," he said, chuckling as she tried to brush the dirt off her pants.

"Where? Why sunset?"

When her grandfather didn't answer, Iris looked up from her fussing to see a shiny silver car in the driveway near the house. A man and a woman were standing nearby, talking to Adele.

"Who are they?" Iris asked, wondering why her grandmother was glaring at them, her arms crossed tightly in front of her.

Her grandfather grumbled again and drove the cart up close. Iris could hear Darby barking and whining in the house.

"Kelly," he said, acknowledging the woman first and then the man, "Brad."

"Good morning, Charles, and happy holidays to you," the man beamed, holding out his hand. The woman was smiling and holding out her hand, as well. Grandfather didn't shake their hands and didn't smile back. Iris had never seen a woman wearing so much make-up.

"Pleasant weather, isn't it?" the man said, still beaming, but drawing back his hand. "It's good to see you up and around, Charles. And who is this lovely young la…"

"I have asked why you've come back here again," Adele cut him off, "since we have made our decision very clear."

The beaming smile dimmed a bit and Iris noticed that, unlike her grandfather and Eric, this man's smile never reached his eyes.

"What a pleasant surprise to see you looking so well, Charles," said the woman. "How are you feeling these days?"

"You're not up for re-election, are you Kelly?"

She laughed loudly at Charles's quip, even though he wasn't smiling himself.

"We've come to discuss our previous offer," said Brad. "We'd love to have the opportunity to tell you more about the new development being proposed. It really does mean wonderful things for the entire county, but there are a few, well, issues that still need to be worked out."

"Before you and Miss Kelly get your interfering asses out of here, would you mind explaining what this has to do with us?" Charles said, and Iris, startled at his rudeness, choked back a giggle.

"Now, Charles, really," started Brad, the smile dimmed even more, "we --."

"We've come with a firm proposal to buy your land," Kelly all but snapped, almost as though she was relieved she didn't have to pretend to be polite anymore.

Iris gasped. Sell the land? The *farm*?

Her grandfather scowled at the two in front of him and there was certainly no twinkle in his eyes now, they were narrowed and his mouth was set so that the lines that framed his rather stern mouth were even more distinct.

He was very pale, too, Iris noticed and put her hand on his arm. "Grandpa...?" she whispered.

The woman glanced sharply at Iris with a strange expression on her face.

"We have made it very clear," her grandmother repeated. "We are *not* interested in selling, no matter what amount is offered."

"It's a *good* offer and one that you'll be very sorry not to accept."

"Your 'offer', as you put it, Kelly, comes off more as a threat." Her grandfather said, getting off the cart. "I think it's time you left and don't bother coming back. You can tell that to your cohorts on the commission as well."

The three of them watched as the two got into the car and didn't speak as it purred past them down the drive.

Iris looked up when she heard her grandfather give a short laugh. He was looking down at her and she saw that her own arms were crossed now, just like her grandmother's.

"An expression like that from one Gibson is bad enough, but I think they've just gotten a double hex from the two of you. Now, lass, help me take care of your tree and then we'll obey orders and go inside."

Charles drove the cart into the shed and told Iris where to go to fill up a watering can. When she came back, he was still sitting in the cart, resting his forehead against the steering wheel.

"Grandpa?" she whispered.

"I'm all right, just a bit dizzy," he said, raising his head and giving her a tired kind of smile. "Bring that damned chair over for me, would you? And lass," he added, with a wink, "not a word to your grandmother or she'll confine us to quarters!"

Chapter Fourteen

WHEN THEY WENT INSIDE, the air was already rich with the aroma of roasting turkey. Charles went to take a rest before Adele could scold. Iris was on her way to wash up and change clothes when Adele called out, "How about helping me make an apple pie this afternoon, Iris?"

Iris stopped in mid-stride and looked around, "Okay!"

"Very well, then, go get cleaned up and we'll get started."

When she came into the kitchen, Iris saw her grandmother putting several green apples into the sink to wash.

"Have you baked very much, Iris?" Adele asked, holding up an apron for her to slip her arms into and then tying it at the back.

"Cookies, mostly, but I helped my mom make pumpkin pies last year. She didn't want to make the crust, though. She said they never turn out for her so she bought the frozen ones."

Adele set Iris about gathering all the other ingredients, because, she said, Iris would be spending time with them and should know her way around the kitchen so she would feel more at home. She found the cinnamon, nutmeg, and salt in a cupboard full of different spices. Flour, sugar, and lard from a large pantry. *Ew,* she thought, *people really eat lard?* The last ingredient was a fresh lemon from the refrigerator.

"These apples came from our own tree in the backyard," said Adele, pushing a cutting board with three of the apples and a small knife towards her and then picked up one of her own. Iris watched as the peel lengthened and fell in one long, curly strip onto the counter.

"My mom can do that, but mine just fall off in little pieces," she said. "Mom heard that if you take the long peel and toss it over your shoulder it will tell you the initial of the person you're going to marry."

Adele laughed. "Now that sounds like some of the old Scottish superstitions from the Highlands and I'm shocked I've never heard of it! But ..." She took up the peel, flung it over her shoulder and it landed on the old linoleum with a clickety-click sound. They both looked down, Iris firmly expecting to see a C for Charles only to see the peel in the distinct shape of a Z.

"Zachariah? Zebulon, perhaps?" Adele said, raising one of her arched eyebrows at Iris and making her giggle.

"Zeke?" Iris suggested.

"Well, whoever he is, we'd better not tell your

grandfather!"

Still giggling, they each picked up another apple and started to peel.

"My mom did that last year and it made an E and the very next week she met Eric!" Iris said, and then her smile faltered as she looked at her grandmother, wondering if she should talk about her mother's second marriage.

Adele seemed not to notice but only smiled as she scooped up the apple slices into a large yellow mixing bowl. At the sound of an engine in the driveway, they both glanced toward the window and a moment later saw a tall, dark-haired young man, shovel in hand, walking past the house.

"Who is *that*?" Iris asked, adding silently, *Wow!*

Her grandmother laughed, "That's Daniel, and he's been helping out around here for most of his life. No doubt Charles has him doing some kind of chore."

Iris reached for another long strand of apple peel and threw it over her own shoulder. She and her grandmother looked down. As hard as Iris searched for a D, there was no discernible letter.

"I think that must mean undetermined, which is just as it should be at your age," Adele said. Peeling another apple, she added, "Your mother sounds like a lovely person and I'm very happy we'll be able to meet again one day soon. Tell me about your stepfather."

As they peeled and sliced and added ingredients, Iris told her about how her mother and Eric had met and how they had gotten married six months later. Adele smiled and didn't seem upset when Iris talked about the things they did together, the movies and his funny imitations and how sometimes she could tell he wanted to get into things when her mom was scolding her, but never did.

"Well then, it sounds as though your mother chooses very well, indeed and I'm happy to hear it.

"Now Iris, take the spatula and just mix it up, see all the juices beginning to settle at the bottom? This is going to be one good pie, if I do say so!"

They talked on while they measured and crumbed, kneaded and rolled out the dough. Iris was amazed at how smooth and flexible the pastry was when her grandmother lifted it from the counter, almost like a piece of cloth.

Adele let Iris scoop the juicy apple slices into the pie plate, and let her roll out the top crust and helped her lift it onto the large mound of cinnamon-sugared apples. Adele showed her how to cut off the extra, pinch it tight along the edges and make some decorative cuts along the top. The finale was to brush the top with cream and dust it with sugar, which Iris did with a flourish.

"Now, you get time off for good behavior, Iris," her grandmother said after they had finished cleaning up and the pie was in the small oven above the large one where the turkey continued roasting. "This will take just about an hour, so do whatever you like for a while. You can look around outside on your own, inside, talk on the phone or watch television. Whatever you want. Just make yourself at home."

After her grandmother left, Iris ate the scraps of leftover pie dough as she walked around the living room, looking more closely at the photographs of her family and the early days of the farm. Iris wondered if her Uncle Alexander lived somewhere nearby and if she would get to meet him soon.

At the bottom of the stairs, she heard her phone and realized she'd left it on the dresser when she changed. She made it upstairs and answered out of breath.

"You promised, Iris," her mother said.

"I know Mom!" she gasped, "Sorry! ... but my hands were... all muddy... when you called the first time, and I left my phone...in the bedroom after I changed clothes... and then Grandmother and I made an apple pie!" she said struggling for breath. "Now it's in the oven."

"I know you're busy, Iris, but this is a weird situation for both of us, so take pity on me and answer your phone when I call. Please?" Iris was relieved to hear a smile in her voice. "Or at least call me back when you can. You can even text me, just as long as I hear from you."

Iris told her about the farmhouse and all the ornaments and her grandmother's cooking and the piecrust and how she had picked out and dug up a spruce tree.

"I remember your dad saying something about a tradition like that," Jennifer said, "planting a tree for each member of the family. Why a spruce tree, sweetheart?"

"It reminded me of ours, the kind we always pick out at the Christmas tree place we go to. This place looks a lot different than that, though!" Iris described the farm, the long rows of different trees and the buildings. "Remember the place we went to pick berries? That's what it looks like, but there's no berry patches, only trees!"

After promising to call her again before she went to sleep, Iris went to her father's desk for his letters and sat cross-legged on the bed to read them. She paused, holding the first one carefully. She had spent the night in his room and the day on the farm, but this seemed different to her, as though she was about to hear his voice for the very first time.

The first ones were a little disappointing, either postcards or very short notes, some just to ask for money or to let them know he wouldn't be home for the weekend or one holiday or another. A few of these short notes and postcards, as well as a birthday card, were to Alexander. By the time his first sophomore semester was ending he wrote that he wanted to come home at Christmas to help during the busy season, and how much he was missing his mother's cooking and sleeping in his own bed. Iris glanced up from the letter to the framed photographs on the wall, now lit up by the bright afternoon sunlight.

This bed, Iris thought, right here in this bed where she was sitting, feeling the now almost familiar tingle, a rush of … of what exactly? The new happiness at seeing her father's pictures, reading her father's words, and sitting in her father's bed, was always followed by a renewed sadness.

When she heard the kitchen timer sound, she bundled up the letters and tucked them back in the desk.

"Wow," said Iris, seeing the golden-brown pie Adele was just setting on the counter.

"There's one problem with this pie of yours, Iris," Adele said, her eyebrow arched in that way of hers. "It might just be too pretty to eat!"

"That might very well be the prettiest one I've ever seen," said Charles, wheeling his way into the kitchen, "but I've *never* seen an apple pie that was too pretty to eat."

While Charles pretended to read a book from a safe distance, Adele and Iris spent the rest of the afternoon making up the mashed potatoes, fixing gravy and cooking peas that had come from their garden.

Her grandmother said that nothing but the best would do for their first real dinner together. Tall white candles in silver candlesticks burned at the center of a table covered with a silky white tablecloth, and several pieces of shiny silverware framed each gold-edged plate.

When dinner was ready and they sat down to the table, Iris wished she had brought something other than blue jeans to wear, but at least her white blouse with the lacy collar and cuffs she had changed into was sort of dressy, she thought, taking her place at the table.

Charles and Adele each held out a hand to her and she reached out shyly and took them in hers. When they bowed their heads, she did the same.

"Heavenly Father," began Charles, "we give our thanks to You for the many blessings You have bestowed upon us. In times that we have suffered through illness, disappointment, and grief, we have been comforted and sustained by our faith in You and the worthwhile and productive work of our hands."

Iris felt her grandfather's clasp strengthen a bit, and after a pause, he continued. "Thank you, Lord, for seeing deeply into our hearts and answering a special prayer. We are profoundly and humbly grateful for the presence of our granddaughter. Amen."

"Amen," her grandmother echoed softly.

Iris whispered her amen as well and lifted her head to see her grandparents smiling at her. Her grandfather gave her a wink and when he let go of her hand, he raised his glass to her and uttered a very long sentence of something in Gaelic that she did not understand at all.

"I don't know what you said, but it sounded really cool."

"That's the first time I've ever heard anyone say Gaelic sounded 'cool'," said Charles, reaching for the knife and sliding the turkey closer to begin carving. "The words mean "May life be showering upon you little one, healthfulness, uprightness and happiness."

Adele uncovered the rolls and passed them to Iris. She felt her face growing warm and wasn't sure what to say except "thank you." It came out too quietly though, and sounded lame to her, especially when her grandmother might have thought it was just for the dinner roll and not for the blessing. But they didn't seem to notice. Adele held a platter as Charles sliced, and soon it was filled with a selection of white and dark meat with a steaming mound of stuffing at the center.

"I know that you and your grandfather will want to play around in the dirt some more tomorrow; he does have a hundred acres to show you, after all," her grandmother said, after taking the rest of the uncarved turkey back to the kitchen. "But I'm driving into Placerville on Sunday afternoon. How about going along with me? I'd love to introduce you and show you around a bit."

"Ah, the teeming metropolis of Placerville, not very impressive when you've traveled all the way from Disneyland," said Charles, with a sort of a snort, and Iris couldn't tell what he thought of either Placerville or Los Angeles.

"If it was up to your grandfather," Adele said, passing the gravy, "he would be like the lairds of Scotland and live right in the center of his vast estate and never leave at all."

"Except to go to war and fight for Bonnie Prince Charlie!" Iris said, and then added seriously to Charles, "Do you know you have the same name as him,

Charles Stewart?"

Another sort of snort. "Lass, there isna' a family tree in Scotland that doesn't have a Charles Edward or a Charles Stewart somewhere along its roots or branches. Where did you learn about that character, anyway?"

This wasn't the reaction she expected, as the books she had read made him out to be the bravest and most loyal of princes. "One book I read about him called him the Prince Over the Water because he had always lived in Italy or France and really wanted to come back to Scotland but the English king didn't want him to."

"Aye, small wonder, and probably the biggest reason that you and I exist today is because our Gibson ancestors were Lowlanders and not quite so caught up in the frenzy as the Highlanders. Your grandmother is descended from Clan MacIntyre, who were Highlanders and many died at Culloden. Sur-rely you read about the gr-reat battle of Culloden?"

"Yes-- aye," Iris answered. "But *sur-rely* you have to fight for what you believe in, r-right?" she added, trying to roll her r's like her grandfather, and remembering how the boy from the book had argued with his father.

"That's true, lass." He grinned at her and added, "but it's a verra good idea to have solid ground beneath your feet and know what kind of army you're up against."

Chapter Fifteen

THERE WERE TWO GARDENS up the hill behind the house, Iris saw as she rode with Charles on the cart. The largest, a square space with long straight rows nearest the house, was a vegetable garden. The other was for flowers and herbs, Charles told her, pointing towards the place near where five tall trees stood sentry behind gray stone benches, and the flagstone path-bordered beds were either cleared down to bare soil or covered with plastic or piles of leaves.

"Here we are, lass," said Charles, stopping the cart near the big trees where there was a freshly dug hole.

"Oh, did Daniel dig this?" she asked. "Grandmother said he's worked here for a long time."

"Aye, he has, and he's wanted me to let him run the place on his own this year, but Adele wouldn't hear of it."

"Why?" Iris asked, hopping out of the cart.

"Because she knows very well I couldn't stand by and not be involved."

"We're all anxious to be open again," said Adele, joining them and sitting down on a wooden bench, holding a large book on her lap. "It just won't seem like Christmas without all the chaos, but we're not going to rush things. You do remember what the doctor said, Charles?"

"Aye, Adele, and I'm sure his advice is very practical, so long as I don't expire from boredom before next season. Now, wee Gibson, if we're to follow tradition, we'll want to have your tree in the ground in, well, about ten seconds."

Charles helped her lower the tree carefully into the hole and she began scooping the fresh soil around the root ball until she was patting it down firmly around the base of the small spruce.

Her grandmother aimed a camera at them and Iris sat up and smiled, and it wasn't hard to smile sitting there with her grandfather's hand on her shoulder. Adele beckoned her over to the bench and she saw the large book was a Bible. Adele used a wide tipped pen at the place where Iris's name and date of birth were already written, carefully adding the date and *Blue Spruce*, each letter carefully formed with her elegant cursive.

Iris looked up as she heard the first notes of a violin. As Charles played, the sun settled farther towards the western hills. The music was quiet and peaceful, almost sad, Iris thought, and it reminded her of one that her mother had wanted her to learn. Jennifer had heard it in a movie and it had made her cry. For her mom, if a song or a movie made her cry, it was good.

Adele set the Bible aside and put her arm around Iris as they listened and watched until Charles finished the last, lingering notes of the song.

"That was lovely, Charles," said Adele, standing up to help him put away the violin.

"May I play something?"

"Of course, Iris. How nice!" said her grandmother, and Iris could almost hear Ashley's voice in her head, *Geez, Iris, when did you get so brave?*

But she had held out her hands and spoken without thinking. *Can't back out now,* she thought, as her grandfather handed her the instrument and her grandmother the bow. All she had to do was remember the notes of the song; it felt strange not to have her music in front of her but after a few squealing false starts, she closed her eyes and played.

The breeze seemed to carry the music over the treetops and across the valley. She played slowly, not rushing through like she did during practice. It felt right to her, to hear this music out in the garden, surrounded by the cool pine-scented air. As she finished and the last of the notes faded, she opened her eyes and saw that the music had the same effect on her grandmother as it always did on her mom.

"Beautiful, Iris. Just beautiful," said Adele, wiping tears from her eyes.

"And here I was thinking I was the best fiddle player in this family. Well done, lass!"

Sunlight was gone from the hillside now and they were in shadow as they all rode the cart back to the house, Iris now sitting cross-legged in the back. She hopped out before they reached the shed and held open the doors so Charles wouldn't have to stop.

"Look at that, Adele. Only here a day and the lass is already reading my mind."

"One day exactly, as I recall," added Adele, helping Charles into his chair, "when the bus driver called to give you up!"

After cleaning up again, Iris was back in the warm, brightly lit kitchen where Adele was putting out the dishes to serve the apple pie. Before it was cut, the cooks posed with their creation, another photo for posterity.

Adele dished up generous helpings in shallow bowls, and they sat along one side of the table with Iris in the middle. She watched as both Charles and Adele poured cream over theirs.

"It's very good, Iris. Try some?" Adele asked, with the small pitcher poised. Iris nodded, and Adele poured just a little bit. When Iris took a bite, she could only nod for her grandmother to keep pouring.

"We thought you might like to see some of the family pictures, Iris," said Adele, as Charles opened a large photo album. The first pictures were of Charles and Adele before they got married. Her grandmother rattled off the names of so many aunts, uncles, and cousins that Iris knew she would never keep them straight unless she wrote them all down. Empty blocks on her family tree would no longer be a problem.

A formal wedding picture with several people on the gray stone steps in front of a church, two bridesmaids in identical pale blue gowns on one side and groomsmen wearing kilts of different colors on the other. Her grandfather was dressed in the now familiar Gibson plaid, a formal black jacket with lots of silver buttons, and a black bow-tie. Her grandmother was smiling radiantly, and beautiful in a shimmering white gown, and Iris finally realized what her mother meant by the word striking.

"Do you see that somewhat bewildered looking character in a skirt next to Herself, who didn't know how he got so lucky?" Charles nodded towards the picture with a wry smile, but Iris could see pride twinkle in his eyes.

"I think you're very handsome," said Iris and Adele at the same moment, making them both laugh. Charles shook his head at them and turned the page.

The next section was all California, pictures of freshly plowed fields, the construction of the new barn and addition to the old house, and pictures of gnarly old apple trees, and then fields of tiny evergreen seedlings.

Baby pictures came next, her father as a tiny newborn, wrapped up snuggly in a teddy bear blanket. In another he was dressed in a rather frilly gown, and looking rather cranky about it, Iris thought.

"Who is Aurora Jean?" She asked, seeing a small group of baby pictures, one with five-year-old Andrew holding a small bundle of pink. Iris was sorry she had asked when her grandparents were quiet for a moment and she noticed that her father's expression was somber, not unlike Alexander's in his picture with her in the little rosebud frame.

"Little Aurora was born with a heart problem, Iris. She lived only a very short time."

"Oh." Iris didn't know what to say, but remembered her mother saying that people ought to say something kind, not just turn away because they couldn't think of just the right thing. "That's so sad."

"Yes it was, but we had Andrew and in a few years Alexander came along."

After several pages of her father—posed school and church photos, baseball and basketball team pictures, and in every season, working on the farm, there were new baby pictures and some of the older Andrew holding baby Alexander.

"If Aurora was a whisper, then Alexander was a shout," her grandmother said with a smile.

Charles nodded, adding, "Nearly eight years between them, but the little scamp was determined to tag along with his big brother."

"As soon as he was walking, he was chasing after Andrew like a happy and very pesky little puppy."

As they grew, there were pictures of them playing, sleeping, eating and working together. Charles and Adele appeared in a few pictures, but mostly it was all boys.

"Where is Alexander now?" Iris asked, turning to the next page that had a lot of little pictures of the boys working around the farm. When neither Charles nor Adele answered, she looked up at her grandfather. Charles made that funny, growly sound he made when he was annoyed.

"Alex lives way over in Pennsylvania," Adele said, standing. She began to clear dishes from the table, but motioned for Iris to stay when she began to get up to help, "He's promised to come for a visit in the spring."

"Went away to college back East to learn all there is to know about growing trees in California. Met a lass whose family owns one of the biggest tree farms in the state, and then, so much for coming home," Charles said, with the same sort of growl in this voice, but Iris could hear the sadness, too.

"Kind of like you, when you left Scotland after you married Grandmother," Iris said, glancing up at him with a smile.

Her grandfather looked stern for a moment and Iris's smile began to fade. From the kitchen, she heard her grandmother stifle a laugh, and then the twinkle lit his eyes again and he reached out and tousled Iris's hair.

"Aye, lass, kind of like that."

"Alexander *did* offer to come home for the season," said Adele, "but even with his help, the doctor advised us that the demands of being open would be too much for Charles. So, it only made sense that he stay to help Janna's family this year.

"Well, look at this," Adele said, pointing to the top of the page and Iris could tell she was trying to change the subject. "I don't think we'd been outside for five minutes and the boys were covered in dirt!"

Iris liked those pictures, Charles on a tractor, or all of them planting seedlings, the boys watering, pruning and cutting the different types of trees, and in some, it seemed as though they were watering themselves more than the trees.

In the photographs taken during the Christmas season, the area between the house and road took on the appearance of a bustling city street during the holidays. Windows were decorated and lit, even on the sheds. Adele stood on the steps of a small building next to the barn holding a tray of cookies, and a sign next to the entrance read "The Emporium." Cars filled the parking lot and people were shown laughing, talking, and working. Iris wished the farm was open this year so she could be a part of it all.

"Next year, Iris, you'll have to come back and be with us for part of the Christmas rush," said Adele, seeming to understand why Iris's gaze rested so long on the busy pictures. "It really is a whole different world. Hard work, for sure, but a lot of fun as well."

The album ended with a Christmas tree.

"The boys always wanted a big tree. Charles could barely fit the angel on top."

The boys were gazing up at the tree. From her tour with her grandfather earlier in the day, she already recognized the Scots pine, its long-needled boughs laden with ornaments, garlands of popcorn and cranberries and silver icicles. Andrew was slender and a head taller with tousled hair and Alexander was rather plump with close-cropped hair in the same vivid shade and they wore the same green plaid pajamas.

Her grandmother closed the photo album and declared it was time for them to get to bed. As Iris started upstairs, Charles said, "It's been quite a day because of you, wee Gibson." He held open his arms and she leaned down to hug him and felt his strong arms hug back.

Chapter Sixteen

THE NEXT MORNING STARTED out rainy and gray, a steady trickle streaming from the gutter outside the kitchen window. And oatmeal for breakfast.

"To pay for yesterday's sins of bacon and gravy and pie with cream," Charles said glumly, as he served Iris a bowl of the thick, steaming mush. The texture and color wasn't anything like the packages she opened and poured hot water over on most school mornings.

"Oh hush," scolded Adele, "you like your porridge well enough. Here, Iris, sprinkle just a bit of sugar or cinnamon sugar over the top."

It was thicker and heavier than her usual oatmeal, but Iris decided that she liked it, especially with the cinnamon sugar.

"Your grandfather is a bit dour this morning, Iris," said Adele, sitting beside her and taking a sip from a steaming cup of amber-colored tea, a thin slice of lemon floating on the top. "In fact, I feel a bit dour myself. Rain or shine, snow or sleet, this would have been one of our busiest days of the season."

Iris wasn't sure what to say. She had seen that they were both upset about something, and was relieved it wasn't about her. Her grandmother looked out of the window and they were all quiet for a few minutes. She kept eating her oatmeal.

"What would you be doing right now if you were open?"

"Well, to begin with, this breakfast would have happened hours ago."

"Jerry, Daniel and I would be making sure we had enough trees stocked in the barn and enough supplies on the shelves ready for the day."

"My friend Fran and I would be setting out baked goods and re-stocking the ornaments and other decorations on the store shelves before opening time."

Charles served himself a second helping, and Iris as well when she held out her bowl. "Once we find a warm sweater and some rain gear for you, we'll go back outside and investigate the other side of the farm."

Iris thanked him for the oatmeal and added, "I knew it was going to rain hard today but I hoped we could still go outside again."

"Checking the weather forecasts on your wee phone, lass?"

Iris shook her head. "Sometimes I just know things. Mom says I can tell the future." She looked up, laughing, "and that she just wished it worked as well on lottery numbers as it does for weather!" She had tried to make her mom understand that the knowing was stronger than ever when she said she had to meet her grandparents. She was hurt that Jennifer didn't understand or trust her knowing, which is what they always called Iris's feelings about some things. She sprinkled just a bit more sugar over her second helping and remembered something in her research, "I read about something called the Sight when I was studying about Scotland. Is that like telling the future?"

Her grandmother looked startled, and as though she *did* know something about the Sight.

"Well, yes, Iris, I suppose it is. You learned about some interesting things as you worked on your project. What else did you learn about Scotland?"

Iris lifted her spoon. "I learned that oatmeal is one of the favorite foods—but what the heck is haggis, anyway?" she asked.

Charles groaned, a spoonful of oatmeal halfway to his mouth. "Please tell me that's not a request for the cook!"

"I don't know. Isn't it good? I didn't think it could be with a name like that."

"Aye, lass. You're right about that," Charles chuckled.

Adele tsked at him again but smiled. "Haggis is called a *savory* pudding – not a *sweet* vanilla or chocolate pudding like you're used to... and the thing to remember about haggis is that in the old days, people used *all* parts of an animal for clothing, tools and cooking," she paused and smiled again at Iris, who felt like she was getting ready to taste haggis instead of just hearing the details. "But many, not including your grandfather, obviously," her grandmother said, after sharing her knowledge of the preparation of haggis, "enjoy it or at least include haggis in their holiday feasts as an important tradition."

A knock on the door interrupted the process of getting Iris bundled up in one of her grandmother's thick wool sweaters and a big green raincoat before they were allowed outside to tour the other side of the farm.

Charles pulled a wool hat down over Iris's eyes and watched as she slowly pulled it back, giving him a playfully glowering look through her veil of tousled red hair. She blew it up out of her face and it fell back, again and again. They were both laughing when Adele opened the door.

"Dr. Alford," Adele said, gesturing for him to come in.

What the hell does he want? Charles was on his guard suddenly, unwilling to let anyone interrupt his time outside with Iris.

"Glad to see the increased dosage has helped, if you're able to get up and about again, Charles. I would caution you, though—"

"No need," Adele said, holding up her hand. Charles knew she was running interference for him, and let her. "I've got them both on a very short leash!

But you haven't met Iris. Iris, this is Doctor Alford."

The doctor looked at her for a long moment before nodding to her. Charles was surprised to see that Iris's expression appeared as guarded as he felt. Glowering in fact, but this time not playfully, he could see she was truly upset. She had been all smiles and impeccably polite with them since her arrival, even when she had to face the music and call her mother. Now, he watched his granddaughter tuck her hands in the floppy sleeves of the raincoat as Alford moved to extend his hand.

The doctor flushed at the rudeness, his eyes narrowing just slightly before nodding to her instead. "So nice to finally meet you, Iris."

"Hello."

Charles saw Adele's eyebrows rise, and caught her eye as the doctor turned away to take something from the bag he carried. More bloody pills, Charles thought, when he could see the now familiar orange bottle. "A new prescription, to replace the ones you have now."

"Stronger?" Adele asked, taking the bottle from him and examining the label.

"A very slight increase—we don't want a repeat of what happened last month," the doctor assured them.

"God forbid," Charles muttered. "Come along, wee Gibson, these two can carry on their conversation better without me."

Her grandfather wheeled himself toward the door. Iris glanced at her grandmother, received a worried smile and an almost imperceptible nod, and followed him out.

It wasn't exactly raining anymore, more like misting, Iris thought. She loved how the clouds touched the tallest of the trees and the raindrops clung to the needles like little teardrops.

"It smells good out here," she said, inhaling deeply when they stopped near a row of tall fir trees. "It really does smell like Christmas trees!"

"Scots pine and Balsam fir are what we would have harvested the most this season," Charles said, indicating the tracts of trees on the lower end of the farm.

At the end of one row, they stopped at the fence and watched a family of deer browsing along the edge of a narrow, rocky creek. So different from the farm, this land was covered with tall, yellow grass, oak trees with their sprawling, twisted branches, and big gray moss-covered boulders scattered across the rolling hillside. The only pine trees weren't pruned and sculpted Christmas trees, but tall and spindly, the ground beneath them littered with dry needles and pinecones. Short tufts of green showed through the tall, dry brush and along the edges of the stream. As they sat and watched, rain began to patter on the cart's canopy and then turned into a steady drumbeat.

"At least the rain nourishes the trees and animals, and will help the grass to grow green again. It's been a dry autumn."

"Do you own that land, Grandpa?" Iris whispered.

"That belongs to Dr. Alford. His house is further up the creek. You met his daughter Kelly yesterday."

"You mean the nasty one with all the eyeshadow and the fancy car?"

He chuckled as he put the little cart in gear. "You are a canny observer of both people and automobiles, wee Gibson."

Charles drove back up to the house through tracts of blue spruce and thick Douglas fir she hadn't seen before. At the driveway, he had Iris open the barn doors and drove inside. This was where cut trees were usually displayed and sold for those who didn't want to venture out into the lot to cut their own.

Gray light filtered in through high, dusty windows, dimly illuminating the vast, empty space, the hand tools that hung on the walls and the spools of thin rope and colorful netting. To one side, a long counter separated the open barn from a sort of workshop, with large cupboards and several drawers labeled for things like wreath frames and hangers, baler netting, and tree stands. Towards the back of the barn were several cone-shaped gadgets of different sizes, each one on its own stand.

"What are these, Grandpa?" she asked, poking her head through the largest one.

"That's a baler, lass," he answered, "and if your grandmother wouldn't be so vexed with me, I'd bale you up in some of that red netting so you couldn't get away."

Her face growing warm, Iris did a somersault through the baler and down onto the dirt floor. "Now I'm baled up with invisible net," she said, sitting up and smiling at him. "That means I can go away, but I'll always come back!"

Chapter Seventeen

AGAIN PUSHING THE LIMITS of their deadline, Iris and Charles were leaving the barn and on their way back to the house when they heard a loud rumbling engine and the sound of tires splashing through puddles in the driveway. Daniel's truck pulled up close to the house, branches of a large tree bouncing with each bump in the road.

"I asked him to choose and bring in a tree for us today, and his Dad has come with him. We can't have you spending your first Christmas with us and not decorate a Christmas tree!"

Iris saw Adele holding open the door, smiling, as Daniel carried in a large tree, a blue spruce, Iris could now recognize, even from a distance. Another man, tall with black hair, just like Daniel, walked towards them.

"Hello, Jerry. Meet my granddaughter, Iris. Iris, this Jerry Lazarro."

"How do you do, Iris?" said Mr. Lazarro, holding out his hand to her.

Although he smiled when they shook hands, Iris could see that he seemed worried.

He turned back to Charles, "I'm afraid I might have some bad news for you, Charles," he said. "We'd like to talk with you and Adele for a while, if you're up to it."

Charles nodded. "Verra well, Jerry, you go on in with Adele and we'll be along."

"What's the bad news do you think, Grandpa?" Iris asked, watching Jerry walk towards the house.

"Hard to say, lass. More than likely some new intrigue about the local power mongers," he answered, reaching up to latch the barn door.

Iris was curious about the news Mr. Lazarro and Daniel brought, but wondering whether she should stay or go to her room when her grandmother beckoned her to the table and moved a steaming cup of hot cocoa towards her with a smile.

"I know we all thought this business was finished," Jerry said, "but it looks like some people, including a couple of the commissioners, have kept this thing percolating behind the scenes. The Sierra Recreation Group are not only planning to open up access to the High Creek Reservoir area, but along that access build shops, and restaurants and even a hotel. You know the commissioners have to be chomping at the bit to get their hands on that kind of revenue."

"That's verra interesting, Jerry," said Charles, looking confused, "but I still don't understand how they think they can get their hands on the place if we won't sell."

Daniel shifted in his chair again. Iris had been watching Daniel while Jerry was talking and the few times he glanced up, she saw that he had very interesting gray eyes. He also seemed to find it hard to sit still, his leg bounced up and down and he shifted position every few seconds.

"I'm glad you called me when you read this, Adele," said Jerry, pushing some papers towards them that Iris recognized as her research. "The few commissioners that have been in on this have been closed-mouthed about their plans—pretty unusual for our local pack of politicians. When I called Howard Haines he said that more and more folks are being put into this position, good, honest, hard-working people who just want to hold onto their homes."

"What position is that?"

"What we're worried about, Charles, is that you won't have to sell, they may be able to just take it."

"What the hell do you mean 'take it', Jerry? This is the United States of America, not...," he paused, glancing at Iris, "not eighteenth-century Scotland!"

Iris jumped when Daniel hit his fist so hard on the table the dishes rattled, "Eminent domain!" he almost shouted.

Iris remembered the night of the Internet search, Ashley saying, *it doesn't sound like anything is really happening, but I'll print it out ....*

No one spoke. Iris looked at her grandparents,

both appeared equally shocked by Daniel's outburst. Adele looked as though she was about to scold him, but Charles was again very pale. Daniel was now still, but Iris knew he was so angry that he wanted to hit something else, or someone.

"I'm afraid that's right," Jerry said. "They'll justify taking your place, not paying you nearly what it's worth, and they'll claim it's for the 'greater good'."

"Eminent domain?" echoed Adele, "I know it was mentioned in the article, but that's for public highways, isn't it? It's not for some fancy private development where just a few people stand to get rich!"

"Well, I'm afraid that's not always the case, Adele. From what Howard said, it seems that some local governments have been stretching the definition of the eminent domain laws, and right here we have people with a little power and a lot to gain. Some have an awful lot to gain," he added, shaking his head. "The Sierra Recreation Group is big, too. Fighting them, especially with enough of the commissioners on their side, will be like David fighting Goliath."

Iris followed when her grandmother got up from the table and went into the kitchen where Adele stood by the sink looking out of the window

"Who's Howard Haines, Grandmother?" Iris whispered. When she didn't answer, Iris looked up and saw that her grandmother was fighting back tears. She put her hand on Iris's shoulder and they stood together for a moment. Iris had a feeling it wasn't like her grandmother to cry much, at least not in front of anyone.

"Howard is an attorney and a good friend. Would you like more cocoa, Iris?"

"The justification," Jerry was saying when they sat back down at the table, "comes from taking an area of land that is not bringing in much revenue, and replacing it with something that could, potentially, bring millions to the local government and economy."

The group was silent. The only sound was the rain falling outside and the water simmering in the kettle on the stove.

Charles cleared his throat. "Not that the farm could possibly compete with something like that, but will they use the fact that we're closed this year against us?" It was the first time he'd spoken since Daniel's outburst.

"It certainly won't help, Charles. The fact that you're closed will give them that much more ammunition."

"If you open right now, today, I'll run it for you," said Daniel, leaning eagerly toward Charles.

For the first time since they sat down, the three adults smiled, but Iris could tell Daniel was very serious. She looked from Charles to Adele, waiting to hear what they would say.

"Ta, lad," said Charles, laying his hand on the boy's shoulder. "But before I take on the county commissioners, unknown corporate giants, not to mention my wife, I think we should go and see

Howard, and find out where we stand."

"Already arranged, Charles," said Jerry. "Howard asked if we could meet here tomorrow afternoon."

After Jerry and Daniel left, the rest of the afternoon passed quietly, except for the rain that sometimes beat down so hard it flowed like a fountain over the rain gutters. Charles and Iris didn't need any encouragement to stay inside. He even went for his required rest without a grumble.

On her way upstairs, she passed by her grandparent's room and heard them talking.

"I'll be damned if I'll take anymore, Adele. Three doses I've missed since the lass arrived, and I feel *better*, not worse."

"But that could just be because Iris is here. That doesn't mean you don't need your medication!"

"If I feel worse, I'll take them; otherwise I'll wait and see the quack again in a few weeks."

"I'm sure Dr. Alford appreciates your high regard."

Quack? Iris thought, walking up to her room, wondering why her grandfather would call his doctor a quack.

"Really, Charles," his wife said, in that intractable way of hers, "You simply cannot stop taking your medication. There could be serious consequences. Let me —"

"No." He hadn't wanted to tell her. Not because he didn't want to share something so important, but almost as though he was afraid the Almighty would change His mind...

"Charles—"

"Adele. Sit."

He patted the bed next to him, and she sat. He reached over and pulled open the nightstand drawer, took out the blue silk pouch and put it in her hand. She withdrew the rosary and held it gently; he knew she was remembering that long-ago afternoon at the church. She looked up, questioningly.

"I prayed, Adele, prayed for a sign—something, anything, to show me I'm not going crazy—that I'm not dying and that those bloody pills are making me worse, not better."

After forty years he had finally succeeded in surprising her, he saw with some amusement.

"You *prayed*?"

"On my knees. And not even on your luxuriously padded pray-do over there, but with my knobby knees on the cold, unforgiving floor."

Her lips quirked in amusement. "That will be the Presbyterian in you."

"Do you remember the lass telling us how she found those adoption papers and knew she *had* to find us?" Adele nodded, and he continued, "I asked her if she remembered just when that was and she did—it was the same night and almost exactly the same time that I prayed. What do you say to that?"

She looked at him for a long moment, then took one of his hands in hers, set the rosary in his palm and closed his fingers around it. "I say, for now, no more bloody pills for you."

Iris knew it was time to call her mom but she didn't feel like talking and sent a short text instead, promising to call later. Iris sat at her father's desk, hands cupping her chin and looking out at the area she and her grandfather had explored that morning, wondering if the deer family still browsed near the stream.

Gray tendrils of mist wove in and around the tall, dark spires of evergreens. It just wasn't possible that anything could happen to this wonderful place, she thought, not after she had just found it, not after she had just found her grandparents. From what Jerry had said, she knew her grandparents would be paid for their land, she knew they wouldn't be homeless or anything, but it was so unfair. Even after these few days she knew they belonged here and couldn't imagine them anywhere else.

She took out the bundle of her father's letters again, untied the ribbon and read the last few. He wrote about dating someone named...Susan? Wow, she thought, I wonder if Mom knows about *that*? But in the very next letter a month later, he wrote that he was dating a girl named Jennifer.

Two letters later he was telling them that he and Jennifer were married. Wow, that was fast, Iris thought. The announcement was followed by an apology, directed at his mother, for not having a church wedding.

Iris suddenly felt like she was spying on her mother, as if she was delving into deep, dark family secrets. But everything that her father wrote about was good news. He'd complain sometimes, but only about a teacher, or his job at the café.

She held her breath as she read his letter announcing that a baby would be born in May. In that letter, there were pictures of her mom and dad that she had never seen before.

She looked closely at the pictures of her mom. Her face young and happy, and her brown hair was so long it almost reached her waist. In the one picture of them together, her mom was wearing a blue jean kind of dress and her father was standing behind her, their hands interlaced on her belly. Wow, thought Iris, that's *me* in there! It was the only picture she had ever seen of them together, and the only picture she had seen of her mom pregnant. She felt another strange tingly feeling in her stomach.

His last letter was dated almost a month before her birthday.

'Sorry I haven't written lately, and thanks for the check, Dad. I must admit to

using just a bit to treat my wife to dinner out on Saint Valentine's Day. I knew you would see that as an investment in my future happiness! Thanks, Mom, for sending the cake—I love you back.

It was great to be home at Christmas – it didn't seem so much like work this year, I guess being away for a while made the difference. I wish Jennifer had just come home with me to meet you both and spend Christmas with us. Jennifer's visit with her mom in Seattle didn't go so well, and she hasn't admitted as much to me, but I sometime wonder if she was abused as a child. Now, her mother has objected to Jennifer getting married, and had the nerve to suggest that Jennifer divorce me and have an abortion! How's that for a welcome home and Merry Christmas? The woman's a nightmare. I seriously doubt if Jennifer will ever see her again.

Which brings me to my next news—and I can see you shaking your head when you read this, Dad, and a very slight "I knew it" smile on your face, Mom. I want to bring Jennifer and the baby home to live once we've graduated. I haven't talked to Jennifer about it yet, but I know she'll agree, especially once she gets to know all of you. I'd like to build that house on the northeast corner of the property like you once offered, Dad.

At first college life, even city life, was great. Just the classes, studying and working in the café a few hours a week was nothing to planting, pruning, cutting, watering or hauling trees almost every day! But lately, especially thinking about the baby and what it would be like to grow up in this environment of endless pavement, crime and smog, rather than in the fresh air and freedom of the farm, I know he or she, would miss out on the best childhood there is.

Also, I want to be there, I want to hang out with Alex and I want to keep The Family Tree in the family. Mostly, Mom, I want you to share all you know about cooking with Jennifer ... but you must never tell her I said that!

Baby's timing is perfect, right after the end of the semester. I must admit our minds have been more on names, layettes, and Lamaze than on school! Once we have some practice being parents, we want to drive up in June and stay for a few weeks. I want to show Jennifer the farm and be on hand for some of the summer work.

This letter must be one-of-a-kind, admitting you were both right and not even asking for money. Well, at least this time, no guarantee on the next one!

We'll be moving in the next week or so. I'll write with our new address and phone number soon.

Love, Andrew

And then there was no more. Anything else that she knew about her dad were the few things her mother and grandmother had told her. Her father was killed by a drunk driver one night on his way home from a late shift at work. Her mother's grief led to an early, difficult labor and a premature birth for Iris.

No wonder her mom didn't want to see or talk about her own mother. If she'd had her way, Iris thought, I wouldn't even exist! Now she understood the expression on her mom's face whenever she talked about family.

With an ache in her chest and throat, she looked at the picture of her mother and father until tears blurred their image, and she lay down on her father's bed and cried.

Chapter Eighteen

SHE WOKE UP LATER in the afternoon, dusky light filtering in through the raindrops on the window, the sound of rain on the roof and her cell phone vibrating on the nightstand. A soft, thick blanket covered her. She reached out and read the message from her mom.

Dinner was a very large turkey pot pie, browned flaky crust, brimming with turkey, vegetables and gravy and as delicious as everything Iris had eaten during her visit. Conversation wasn't as easy, every subject seemed to lead to talk of trees or family, and hovering at the edge was the reality of losing the farm.

Iris helped her grandmother clear the table and load the dishwasher.

"We'll decorate the tree now, Iris," said Adele, closing and switching on the machine, and then added with a smile, "and maybe you could help your grandfather untangle the lights? He *might* not curse quite so much if you're helping."

While helping, and giggling at her grandfather's cursing and her grandmother's scolding, Iris noticed that the strings of lights were just like the ones that she and her mom liked, the big clear bulbs in bright colors. There were also several different bulbs that had tubes of colored water attached that her grandmother called bubble lights. Once the lights were attached to the branches the way her grandmother insisted, they stood back and surveyed the tree and Iris could see a few of the lights begin to blink here and there, and the water in the tubes start to bubble.

"Something's missing," Adele said, searching the tree with a frown.

"Ornaments perhaps, Adele? They're still in the box behind you."

She gave him a look that made Iris giggle again. "No, it's something else...before the ornaments..."

"I know!" Iris cried, "Popcorn and cranberries!"

Her grandparents turned to her in surprise.

"That's right, Iris! How did you know?"

"The pictures of your trees in the photo albums," she answered, "and my mom and I do that too, sometimes."

"Well, we can't stop to pop and string popcorn tonight, so it's on with ornaments," Adele said, kneeling beside the big box that held the ornaments.

"Oooh!" Iris breathed when Adele opened the lid. Each one was different and tucked into its own little niche. Adele lifted one out gently and handed it to her. "How about making this one the first, my dear?

Beautiful, isn't it?"

Iris took the delicate lavender glass ornament and saw that it was an iris.

"Just like you, wee Gibson. How about right here?"

Iris touched the smooth petals and then reached up to hang the iris in the soft golden light. Several angels, Holy Families and Three Kings, cherubs, birds, bells, flowers, Santas, candy canes, snowflakes, and icicles followed until the tree was full and the box empty.

They sat back on the couch with the Christmas music playing softly in the background, enjoying leftover pie and cream.

"Grandpa, what will you do if... well, if they make you sell this place?"

"Well, lass," he said after a few moments, "I never thought of doing anything else. But after today with all the cold rain and fog, I say we try something warmer if it comes to that. Macadamia nuts on Maui, how would that strike your fancy?"

He wasn't smiling that Iris could see, except when she leaned around, she could see the twinkle in his eyes.

Adele answered as seriously, "No Charles, I think warmth and a change of holiday might be in order. Easter Lilies on Bermuda?"

They spent the next few minutes imagining more and more outrageous crops and exotic locations until they all laughed at Iris's final suggestion of

"Coconuts in the Caribbean?"

"I don't see how we're going to top that one, do you, Charles?" said Adele, standing up and clearing the dishes, "and I think it's time we got some sleep, early Mass tomorrow."

Iris looked up at her.

"Church," Adele explained with a smile.

"Oh," said Iris, "I don't really have anything nice enough to wear to church…"

"That's all right, lass," said Charles, standing up and waving away his chair when Iris started to get it for him. "I wear my blue jeans every now and again and they haven't thrown me out yet."

"Charles!" Adele scolded. "It's thoughtful of you to be concerned about that, Iris, but it really is all right to wear blue jeans to church if there's nothing else suitable…" she stopped, a thoughtful expression on her face and suddenly set the dishes back down. "Come with me."

In their bedroom, Adele opened a big wooden chest at the foot of their bed. After moving several items, she found what she was looking for. "Here it is. What do you think?" Her grandmother was holding out a plaid skirt and Iris recognized the Gibson plaid at once, but no, it wasn't a skirt, it was a kilt—a real kilt! "Would you like to wear this? We had them made for Andrew and Alexander in Scotland the one time we all visited."

Iris remembered seeing the pictures of the boys dressed up in them in the photo album. Iris held it up

Cynthia Rinear Bethune

to see if it would fit and felt something on her head.

"Tam o'shanter," said Charles, joining them and smiling down at Iris as the tam slipped down over one eye. "You're going to make everyone want to hear bagpipes in that get up, wee Gibson."

"What do I do?" Iris was on the phone to Ashley as soon as the bedroom door closed behind her. "I've never been to a Catholic Church before, but Mom said something about it being different once. Different from what?"

"Beats me, I've never been to any other church. Go in, sit down, well, you should really genuflect— that's something like a curtsy—and cross yourself, but you're not a Catholic so you don't have to do that. Then kneel and pray for a while until you start to hear all the kneelers bang up against the pews – my mom hates that!"

"Okay. Kneel and pray. What else?"

"Sit down until everyone stands up for the priest to come in. Just follow along with everyone else, Iris. I mean, it'll be okay. It's not like they're going to throw you out or anything if you do something wrong! Just don't go up for communion, that's when most people go up and get the bread and wine. You don't do that. Just sit still, pray or sing or whatever."

"Why not?"

"You have to go to classes and a ceremony for the first time. The bread and wine, well, they sort of…well…they represent Jesus in a special way, and you have to go to a lot of classes to understand that, I guess."

That seemed pretty understandable to Iris, but she didn't say so.

The next morning, she walked downstairs after getting dressed and heard a whistle.

"Look at the lass, Adele."

But her grandmother had already seen her, standing there in her green, red and gold plaid and lacy white blouse.

"Oh my dear, aren't you adorable! Your father would be so proud of you, wearing his kilt and tam."

"Did I put it on right?" Iris asked, reaching up to make sure the tam o'shanter wasn't falling off her head again.

"Perfectly, but I'll slip in a hairpin or two so you don't have to worry about it. Now Charles, are you sure you don't want the chair?"

"It's about ten steps to the car, and ten more to the Church, Adele. It's not worth the bother."

The morning was cold, but clearing and the sky was a pale blue, with a few cotton candy-like clouds catching the sunrise by the time they reached the church. It seemed small to Iris, a dark wooden building set back in the trees with a simple sign out front. A winding path led past a manger scene of colorful, carved wooden figurines to the arched double doors.

Along the way, several people nodded and smiled hello.

As they walked inside, Adele whispered to her, "Just follow along with what we do and I'll tell you other things along the way. If you're not sure or not comfortable doing something, just watch and listen and enjoy the service."

Afterwards, when Iris remembered the service, she thought of the stained-glass windows. Trying her best to follow along in the booklet, wondering where the music was coming from and just what the funny sounding words meant, the sun rose higher and shone through the windows on one side of the church. Vibrant, jewel-colored light splashed over the congregation, the priest in his white and rose-colored robes and the lacy white altar cloths.

She stopped trying to follow in the book after that, just followed as her grandparents stood, sat or knelt. During the Lord's Prayer, her grandparents held her hands and afterwards her grandmother hugged her, and said, "Peace be with you, Iris." Her grandfather kissed the top of her head and whispered, "Get ready to have your hand shaken off, wee Gibson." Then it seemed like everyone in church came by to shake her hand, even Father Kevin leaned in with a big smile, grasped her hand in both of his and said in his booming voice, "Peace be with you, Iris!"

When her grandparents returned from communion, they pulled down the padded kneeler and knelt to pray again. Hesitating for only a moment, Iris slipped from the pew onto her knees, too, and bowed her head. She tried to form the words in her head into a real prayer like she had just heard, but it didn't sound right to her. She finally started thinking about how happy she was to have found her family and what she wanted the most; her grandfather to be well, for her grandparents to be able to keep the farm, and for her mom not to be too mad when she got home. She hoped that wasn't too much to ask.

When she heard the kneelers being slammed back into place, she added a hasty *thank you very much, Amen.*

After lunch Charles willingly went for a nap, freely admitting he was tired out after all the walking and visiting at church. Then it was her grandmother's turn to take Iris on a tour, this time into Placerville. As Adele drove, she pointed out different landmarks, businesses, and places where friends lived along the ten miles to town.

"Are there a lot of Christmas tree farms around here?" Iris asked when they passed by a sign advertising another tree farm.

"There are quite a few in the area and it's a wonder we all keep in business. Between the holidays and sales to landscaping contractors like the Lazarros, we all manage. I know that we were joking about other crops and other holidays, but I can't imagine another way of life for us."

"Christmas is my mom's favorite holiday, mine too, I guess," said Iris, smiling at her grandmother, "especially now."

"Regardless of what faith a person is, even if they aren't a believer, the Christmas season offers so much beauty and peacefulness. I know we are blessed to have built our lives around it."

On the outskirts of town, there were a lot of fast food restaurants and a big store that Iris recognized, but Adele passed these by and went into Placerville. Here the shops were smaller and Iris didn't recognize any of the names.

"Now, what do you think of our little town?"

Iris looked around as Adele drove slowly down a small street, "It's nice, just a lot different than where I'm from," she answered, thinking of the mall where she and her mom usually shopped, that was much wider and probably as long as the whole street. She liked the old-fashioned buildings and the interesting bell tower in the center of the town.

"I like to shop at our friends' small, local stores, and they buy their trees at our place. That helps to keep everyone in business."

At every shop, Adele introduced Iris and almost everyone asked how she was enjoying her visit and told her how happy they were to meet her. No one seemed surprised at all that she was suddenly a part of the family. When Iris mentioned this, Adele gave a Charles sort of snort.

"Well, Iris, you and your friend Ashley have the

Internet, but in Placerville we have something that gathers information and spreads news even faster. That would be Mrs. Dietz. Charles says..." she paused and smiled. "Well, never mind about that. Mrs. Dietz is the owner of the diner, so she has all day to give and receive the latest news. We'll go and have some tea or hot cocoa before we go home and make her day."

Shop windows were decorated for Christmas and each store had a different kind of holiday music playing. At a clothing store, her grandmother bought Iris some extra outdoor things, wool socks and warm sweaters, and some black rubber boots that were really ugly, although she smiled and said thank you.

"I know the boots are ugly, but there's nothing like these for keeping your feet warm and dry when you're outside traipsing around with your grandfather," Adele said, and Iris wondered again how her grandmother always knew what she was thinking. "It took hours for your shoes to dry out after your excursion in the rain yesterday. Your poor feet must have been freezing."

At the diner, she and her grandmother took a seat at the counter where Mrs. Dietz stood the entire time they were drinking their cocoa. Other customers, after failing to get her attention, ended up serving themselves coffee, shaking their heads at her as though they were used to it. Gushing over her until she felt red in the face, Iris was relieved when Mrs. Dietz finally changed the subject.

"I couldn't believe it when I heard about the

proposal, Adele dear, running a road right through the center of your place! Where would the town be without The Family Tree up there on the hill? I told Bernie and Jack here the other day; those characters on the commission better just watch themselves. We voted them in and we can vote them right out again!"

Chapter Nineteen

SINCE CHARLES WAS STILL napping when they returned from town, Iris decided to walk down to the creek to get pictures of the deer family.

On the way, she met Daniel cutting up an old wild pine that her grandfather had told her had fallen over in the last windstorm. A chainsaw sat next to him on the bench, and the bed of the cart was stacked high with short, round pieces of wood.

"Hey," he said, tossing the pieces of cut up wood inside the woodshed.

"Hey," she answered, wondering if there was a way to sneak his picture. Maybe from the barn, she thought, watching him for a minute, until he paused and looked up at her.

"You need something?"

Iris shrugged and felt herself blush, but decided to ask the question on her mind.

"Why were you so mad the other night?"

"Mad?"

"The night I first got here, I was hiding behind

the sign when you drove out so fast. My grandmother said it wasn't like you to do that..." she shrugged, "...so...I just wondered..."

He glowered at her and used the sleeve of his shirt to wipe the sweat off his face. Iris noticed how the bright blue plaid shirt made his gray eyes even...nicer.

"My girlfriend broke up with me," he finally answered.

"*Why*?" Iris blurted, "I mean..." she paused, feeling herself blush, again, "Oh."

She saw the twitch of a smile at the corner of his mouth before he turned to start splitting the wood. He set one round on top of the other, swung the axe and she jumped when the four pieces flew apart. He paused, and asked what she was up to. When she explained about the deer at the creek, he shrugged and said they were usually only there early in the morning. "If you're going, you better hurry up. That's a long way to go to be back in time for the meeting."

He said it in a nicer voice, but she knew he didn't want her standing there staring at him or to talk about his stupid girlfriend.

She started down the tract of balsam fir, and then looked back from behind one of the trees to see him putting in earphones and slipping his iPod in his pocket. She raised her phone, snapped a picture, and ran.

The pale sunlight wasn't warm enough to penetrate the thin gray clouds into the rows of evergreens and she shivered, but her feet were *warm* in the thick wool socks and ugly black boots. Each day she had spent on the farm had been different, cold and bright the first day, gray and rainy the next and today somewhere in between. She could smell the wood smoke from the farmhouse chimney, hear the call of chickadees nearby and the distant whine of a saw.

Along the way to the creek she tried to remember all the different types of trees her grandfather had introduced her to. Blue spruce was easy to recognize now, and she remembered the Ponderosa pines had longer needles and were a brighter shade of green, but was this row balsam or Douglas fir?

Finally, at the fence line, she searched for the deer but the only wildlife was a pair of big, silvery gray squirrels, well camouflaged against the trunks of the big oak trees and river rock along the stream. She took pictures of them as they ventured out to gather cones and acorns, and walked along the fence to see if the deer were further upstream.

She wove in and around the different rows, seeing trees she hadn't been introduced to yet. "I'm getting to be just like Grandpa, introducing myself to trees!" she said out loud to herself. "If I knew Gaelic, I could *really* introduce myself."

She made do with reaching out and touching the boughs as she walked by.

As she started down to the creek again to look for the deer, the smell of evergreen, always faintly in the air was suddenly much stronger. She pushed through a row of full sized cedar trees and stopped.

A wide expanse of sky, where tall trees should be standing, opened in front of her.

Charles had told her that one or two trees were stolen each season, usually always from the row nearest the highway. At Iris's gasp of outrage, he gave a chuckle, "Aye lass, it used to make me angry, as well. But your grandmother reckons that anyone who feels driven to steal a Christmas tree must need our prayers more than our anger, and I've come to agree with her."

But this wasn't a poor person trying to give their family a happier Christmas.

Iris's eyes fell to the ground where several fir trees lay, not just cut and taken but hacked to pieces. Iris crept forward and dropped to her knees, reaching out for one of the boughs still attached to its trunk, stroking the soft needles and wishing she did know some way to talk to them. She pulled out her phone. Her first impulse was to call her mother, but what could her mother do? She would only be worried. For the same reason, she didn't want to call her grandparents. Tears came to her eyes imagining her grandfather's face at the sight.

Jerry was due to arrive for the meeting with the attorney. Iris decided to wait and tell them all together what she had found.

As she started to get up, she heard a loud sneeze, followed by laughter and deep voices several rows away, and then chainsaws!

Her mouth went dry but at the same moment

she started towards the sound, cutting across the tracts, hiding behind and peeking through trees until she reached a row of the Douglas fir. That's right, Douglas firs are the really thick ones, she remembered, breathing deeply, trying to swallow and calm her hammering heart. She crept close to one of the biggest, cautiously peeking through the branches and saw two men cutting their way up a long row of Scots pine. Without thinking, she pushed her hand through the boughs, snapped a picture with her phone and took off running up the hill.

She kept running through the rows of trees and away from the noise, so they wouldn't hear her if the chainsaws stopped, thanking her mother with every step for making her enter Sheriff Abbott's number in her phone.

Iris felt a surge of relief when she heard a woman's strong, clear voice. "El Dorado County Sheriff's office."

"Sheriff Abbott needs to come to The Family Tree!" she said in a sort of shouted whisper.

"Iris? What's wrong?" The dispatcher was a lady named Caroline, who Iris had met only an hour ago at the diner.

"There are two men cutting down a lot of trees!"

The dispatcher kept her talking, describing the area of the farm she was at and the description of the men and what Iris had witnessed. Iris looked at the picture but the men's faces were turned from the camera.

Iris was pacing, wishing the Sherriff would hurry. She could hear the woman relay the information and it wasn't long before she could hear the siren over her phone. Iris just hoped it wouldn't scare the men off before they could be caught.

"I'm going to get another picture," Iris told the dispatcher.

"No, Iris! You stay where you are or, if it's safe, run back up to the house. The sheriff will be there in less than five minutes."

"But they might get away!" She was already moving back towards the sound of the chainsaws from a new direction, hoping to get a picture of their faces this time.

"It's okay," she whispered. "They won't see me."

The dispatcher was protesting again, but Iris was moving towards the cedar trees which now separated her from the sawyers. Pushing her way into the wing-like boughs, she was suddenly lifted off her feet.

Chapter Twenty

THE PHONE FLEW OUT of Iris's hand as she struggled against the strong arms holding her, dragging her off into the thick, wild trees that bordered the farm.

"Stop! Iris, it's me! Ouch!" Daniel hissed in her ear just as she bit down hard on the hand over her mouth.

"Ouch!" he hissed again, letting her go and grabbing his hand back, and now pushing her towards the shelter of the trees. "What do you think you're doing?"

"Trying to get a picture of them in case they get away! What are you doing?"

"I heard chainsaws where there shouldn't be chainsaws! I wanted to get you out of here in case there was trouble—"

"Trouble?" Iris almost yelled. "Have you seen what they're doing?"

She ran towards the trees and grabbed up her phone at the same time the chainsaws stopped. Now there was only the sound of a siren wailing in the distance—until Iris took one more step onto dry leaves and twigs. The crackling sound seemed to echo loudly through the air.

She shoved her hand through the boughs, aiming blindly, and took the picture.

Daniel was pulling her back again, and this time she didn't fight. She let him pull her up the hill as fast as they could run, across several rows to keep out of sight.

Finally reaching the grassy slope between the barn and the house, Iris stopped, panting and falling to the ground. Daniel stood next to her, leaning with his hands on his knees, panting and scowling at her.

"*What*?" she said in between gasps, scowling right back. "What if they got away?"

"Did you happen to see that at least one of those guys had a gun?"

A *gun*?

"No. But I'm glad I didn't because then I would have been too scared."

"That's nothing to how scared I would have been, telling your grandparents something had happened to you!"

Still trying to catch her breath, she looked at the picture. Trying to make sense of what she was seeing, she turned to block the light from the screen.

"Oh my God!" she squealed, suddenly breaking into a fit of giggles. She knew by his expression that Daniel must think she'd gone crazy, which only made her laugh harder.

She handed him the phone, trying to control her giggles as she watched him, falling over laughing again when she saw the grin start to spread over his face.

Her blind reach through the trees had caught two men, staring straight into the camera, bug-eyed surprise on their faces. One of them was facing the camera with chainsaw in hand, and the other was bent over, looking back over his shoulder and reaching for his jeans that were halfway down his big, hairy butt.

"Geez, Iris," Daniel said, shaking his head at her. "You are *un-be-lievable!*" Just as she started to catch her breath and stop laughing, he added, "That's going to make one ugly wanted poster!"

"Well, I'll be goddamned," Sheriff Abbott muttered under his breath at the picture when they were finally all inside. "That alone has got to break a law or two," he added with a chuckle as he finished sending himself the photo, and set the phone on the table near Iris. "I just hope it doesn't break your phone, Missy."

Iris wondered why her grandmother was frowning at the Sheriff, but then things had started to go a bit fuzzy around the edges.

The Sheriff pulled out a chair and sat down. "Smooth operators, these two. Once they saw they were on candid camera, they ran to their truck and tried to skedaddle. Trouble is, the Doc's little road has a few too many of those granite boulders and Hairy here managed to hit one and stall out." He shook his head, and added more seriously to Charles, nodding towards the phone. "George Grant, so that mystery is solved, I'm afraid. He'd taken off, but Jensen caught him runnin' over the hill and back towards the highway."

Iris heard their voices, but couldn't seem to stop staring at things, now it was her grandmother's hands. Iris watched intently as Adele stirred a heaping spoonful of sugar into a steaming hot cup of dark red tea and then at the sparkly granules as they slowly swirled and disappeared.

"A good, old-fashioned English cure for shock, my dear. Strong, sweet tea. Drink up."

Charles was sitting next to her with one hand resting on her shoulder. When Iris finally looked up, he winked and lifted his glass to her. "Only because you're too young for the good old-fashioned Scottish cure for shock, wee Gibson."

Shock? Iris had heard about shock before but thought it meant when you were hit by lightning, or when you touched the metal thing on a plug when it was still in the socket. Was that causing the wooziness in her head and the sort of numb, heaviness of her legs? She felt the heat of the cup on her icy cold fingers, and the first sip of tea trickled a warm path all the way down to her stomach.

"Maybe you should pour a bit for me, Charles," Adele said and Charles raised an eyebrow in an Adele-like manner. "Fortification," she answered his look, sitting down next to Iris and laying a hand on her other shoulder. "For when I have to call this child's mother and tell her what happened before she hears about it on the news."

Mr. Haines arrived and the talking went on around her, and she could hear everything but there were still long moments where she couldn't seem to look away from the pattern of tiny blue and gold flowers on the teacup in front of her. A scone with a lot of blueberries, lemony frosting and dollops of whipped cream appeared in front of her and all of a sudden she felt hungry.

"She sees right through me, Iris," Mr. Haines said, winking at her. "Your grandmother knows one of my favorite things on this planet are her lemon blueberry scones!"

Howard, he said Iris could call him, wasn't at all what she expected. He appeared to be quite a bit older than her grandparents and was very tall and thin with a slightly crooked back, but he also wore old blue jeans, a plaid work shirt with rolled-up sleeves, and his gray hair was tied back in a long, stringy ponytail.

At first, talk was just about family and health concerns, and how the law business in town had been quiet lately. "Although, this could certainly shake things up a bit!" he added with a chuckle as he piled the thick whipped cream on his second scone.

Once they turned to business, though, Iris noticed that Howard's behavior changed completely.

When he began to explain the eminent domain law more fully, his eyes were sharp and he looked at each one of them in turn, even Iris, to make sure they understood.

"So, you can see that eminent domain was established for a very important reason and sometimes it *is* reasonable to enforce. But when you have local politicians who are willing to go along with and be bought off by special interests, then the rights of the individual landowners like you are just plowed right over, sometimes before anyone even realizes what is happening.

"With access barred here by the boundary of the national park," he said, pushing on some crooked wire-framed glasses and pointing to an area east of them on the county map, "the only access for this area is right through the center of your farm and would also take most of Doc Alford's place next door. The width of the road, along with the usual rights-of-ways and easements, would impact much of your growing area and therefore your business.

"You're absolutely sure that you have no interest in selling?" he asked, taking off his glasses and wiping the lenses on his shirttail as he looked from Adele to Charles. "I'm sure we could get you a very good price. And, if what I've heard about recent experiences with eminent domain is anything to judge by, you could save yourselves a lot of grief."

"Absolutely not," Adele answered immediately.

The woozy feeling had passed, and Iris waited

for her grandfather's answer. Charles gazed out the kitchen window, and Iris knew that he saw beyond the driveway, barn, and sheds to the rows of trees. Iris shifted in her chair and Charles glanced at her before answering.

"No. We aren't to be forced from our home and our livelihood," he said. "If we decide one day to sell, it will be on our own terms."

Howard surveyed the faces around the table. "The next question is, are you ready for a fight?"

Iris could see that Jerry, Daniel, and her grandmother were all looking at her grandfather.

"At least we know our enemy and have firm gr-round under our feet, don't we Gr-randpa?" she blurted out, again trying to twist her tongue around a Scottish brogue and feeling her face grow warm when all of them turned to her in surprise.

"Aye, lass, that we do," said Charles, a wry smile smoothing out the worry lines on his brow. "On a positive note, whatever happens, canna be as bad as Culloden."

Howard's smile seemed to melt off his face suddenly, "Well, folks, maybe this isn't the time to confess that my ancestors fought on the side of the redcoats in that particular battle, but maybe now …

"Now then, young man," he said, straightening up to attention and addressing Daniel in a clipped British accent. "I commission you to go forth into the heather! Beware Butcher Cumberland, but do not return until the closed for the season sign is down!"

Daniel grinned and jumped up from his chair, but stopped and looked to Charles for permission. Charles nodded and Daniel was out the door.

"Good man! Make a note, Bletchley," Howard said to Iris, still in character, "to put that young whippersnapper up for promotion!"

Then he kind of shook himself. "Now, then, where was I?" he asked, chucking Iris under the chin. "Ah yes, the first priority is to take away the commission's argument, that by being closed, you are not bringing in the usual revenues to the county coffers. They might also argue that if Charles's health does not improve, your business may not reopen in the future."

Iris saw Adele cast a worried glance at Charles.

"I'm not sure we can manage opening this year, Howard. We *do* have Charles's health to consider, we haven't prepared at all and there's less than a week until Christmas..."

"I understand, Adele, but it's not really about how many trees you sell, it's about having the intent to do business. Besides," he added with a smile, picking up papers and maps and putting them back in his briefcase, "I have faith in the Christmas spirit, and I'm sure that anyone who might stop by to purchase a Christmas tree will understand if you don't have every size and variety of tree that you usually do.

"I'll make some calls and find out just exactly where this stands, then we'll know the next steps to take. And, if Abbott can get those two lumberjack-asses to talk, and we can tie in today's trespass and vandalism to whoever's behind this –well then, case closed!" Howard's cell phone rang and he excused himself from the table to take the call outside.

Iris sat at the table, chin resting on her hand and looking out the window, listening to Charles and Jerry talk about the work involved in opening unexpectedly mid-season. She watched as Howard finished his phone call and talked to Daniel and wished she could read lips or hear through walls when she saw Daniel nod and then smile broadly. After exchanging a few more words, Daniel almost ran to his truck and tore out of the driveway even faster than he did the night she was hiding behind the sign. She started when Adele's voice drew her attention back inside.

"Charles, Howard said 'sell a few trees' but you two are talking as though it was a regular season. The doctor said—"

"The doctor said I was to avoid stress. Which do you think would be more stressful to me, Adele, working hard or waiting around for someone else to either help us or ruin us?"

It wasn't the usual arched eyebrow way when she was scolding. Iris could see her grandparents were looking into each other's eyes, almost like they were carrying on a conversation without speaking.

"Well then, since we'll be open, we open the way we always do and I'll do my part as well," said Adele, and she stood and started clearing the cups from the table

Iris carried the tray of scones into the kitchen.

"How are you feeling, Iris?" Her grandmother took the tray and looked closely at her, and Iris could see the worry of the afternoon evident in the creases in her forehead and the tight way she held her mouth. "Maybe you should lie down for a bit?"

"No." Iris shook her head, "I'm okay. The tea really worked!"

"I'm glad, my dear. In that case, could you run out and put this plate of scones in Howard's car? And then, before things get out of hand around here, you had better organize your things for tomorrow...."

Leave tomorrow! How could she have forgotten it was time for her to board the bus back home tomorrow? Her grandparents were driving her to the larger town of Modesto, so she wouldn't have as long a trip and wouldn't have to change buses on her way home. It would take them hours to do that, when they should be here at the farm. When she should be here at the farm, too.

Howard hadn't been gone an hour and already Adele had started to call the seasonal help they usually hired to see if they would be available at such short notice. Sheriff Abbott had his deputies block the scenes of the crime. Daniel had returned with Sean and Hamid, and now they were all out in the tracts of trees with Charles. He wanted to make sure they all knew which trees were to be harvested and brought to the barn for purchase and those that would remain for the customers to choose and cut themselves. Jerry had gone to town for supplies.

Iris was the only one not working. That would have to wait until she made the phone call and this call was going to be even harder than the first, Iris thought. She procrastinated, throwing sticks for Darby and playing tug-of-war with him when he wouldn't give them back, and thought about what she was going to say. Finally, she perched on a fencepost near the barn and called her mom.

"Mom, I need to ask you something really important."

After a pause, she heard her mother sigh.

"What is it now, Iris?"

"I know I promised to come home tomorrow, but I *really* need to stay for a few more days."

Before Jennifer could say no, Iris told her about the threat to the farm.

"No, Iris!" Jennifer finally interrupted, "you can stop right now! You've been gone long enough. You are *really* testing the limits here. Do you have any idea how lucky you are that I let you stay at all? I still don't even know these people, and if…"

"If you did, you'd want to be here, too! This is important, Mom, I really need to help!"

"Iris, you didn't even know them a week ago. How can you expect to help with these complicated business problems?"

"It's not complicated, Mom! They might lose this place because someone else wants to get a lot of money!

It's not fair! And I can help. I can bake and sell things. I can help bale trees. I can babysit little kids when people are here buying trees."

She stopped, not only because she realized she had no idea how to bale trees or bake very much, but also because her voice had started to break and her throat tighten in that "squeak shut" way that her mother called the pain just before tears.

Darby, his whiskers all gummed up with pine pitch, dropped the stick he was chewing and looked up at her, his head to one side.

"I just can't stand the thought of leaving tomorrow…"

"Iris…"

"Please, Mom? It's only a few more days until Christmas."

"I know it is, sweetheart, and that's one reason I want you home. I miss you. We all miss you." After a long pause, Jennifer sighed again. "My God, I don't believe I'm saying this, but …I'll talk with your grandmother again, and if it's okay with her —"

"*Thankyouthankyouthankyou!*" Iris squealed and jumped, nearly falling off the fencepost. "I know it will be!"

"Just for another few days, Iris! No more extensions, no more excuses. Do you understand? You *have* to be home before Christmas!"

Iris was nodding, pulling a paper out of her jacket pocket, "I know, Mom, I promise, but I have one more question."

"God, Iris, now what?"

"It's just about Grandpa's medicine. You know a lot about medicine, don't you? What is Digoxin?"

"I know what Digoxin is, why?"

"Well, Grandpa said he felt better when he forgot to take it the other day. Actually, he said he felt worse all the time when he took it. I was worried, I thought that maybe it was the wrong kind of medicine for his heart. Remember the show we saw on TV that time, about the person who accidentally got the wrong medicine?"

Iris could hear her mom typing on a keyboard. "A lot of medicines can have negative side-effects, honey, that doesn't mean it's the wrong one. I don't know if your grandparents want us nosing around in their business."

"But I don't want to say anything unless I'm sure. I don't think Grandpa would mind, especially if it means he doesn't have to take it."

Another pause, another sigh. "Okay, Iris. Digoxin is a heart medicine, so if that's what he's taking, it should be all right. Did you see what it looks like? Capsules or tablets? Did you notice if it had lines or what was written on it?"

"It's a little white pill with a line, and some letters and numbers." Iris glanced at the little slip of paper and read the information off for her mom.

After a long pause, Jennifer asked, "Do you know if he's still taking them?"

"From what I heard, he said he's not going to

take them unless he feels worse. He said he would go to the "quack" after Christmas. But Mom, he really *is* better. He's walking a lot more now and everything, and he didn't when I first got here."

"Are you sure about the information on them, Iris? Is there any way he might have mixed up two medicines?"

"I wrote exactly what was on the pill, Mom. And Grandpa said it was the only one he took, and that it was one too many. Why?"

"I just wanted to make sure before I check into things. Now, hold on, honey, here's Harry, no Heath…"

Iris held the phone away from her ear while each of the twins launched into some story in that excited four-year-old way of theirs. It even made her miss them a little.

Chapter Twenty-One

WHEN SHE FINALLY HUNG UP after talking to her mom, she heard Christmas music playing softly from a speaker over the barn. She threw the stick for Darby again, wanting to give her mom a chance to talk to her grandmother before she went back inside, and hoping she was right when she had insisted that it would be okay for her to stay and help.

She walked back into the house when her grandmother was just hanging up the phone.

"Thank you, my dear," she said, reaching out to hug her. "It means the world to me that you want to stay and help, and I know your grandfather will feel the same. Are you sure, though? I know you must miss your family, and it *is* a lot of work"

"I'm sure," she said. "I really want to help, and I promised Mom I'd be home for Christmas."

When she hauled cleaning supplies out to the shop, a green and black sign with fancy gold letters had been put up on the door. "The Emporium" was to be back in business as well, her grandmother had said.

Their longtime customers would expect it and they wouldn't drop their standards just because they were forced to open unexpectedly. Adele was already baking a large batch of brownies.

Iris was put to work vacuuming the accumulation of dust from the shelves and counters and floors, and spider webs from nooks and corners. When she finished, Adele and a friend she introduced as Fran came in with buckets and cleaning supplies.

"All right, Iris, you have proven your superior ability at fiddling, baking, and vacuuming," said her grandmother, opening the tap to run hot water into one of the buckets. At first, there was only a loud hissing sound, following by banging and spitting until finally the water started to flow. "Now, let's see how you are with mopping and scrubbing!"

Adele and Fran talked their way through the cleaning and it made the work seem less like work, Iris thought, especially when her grandmother talked about growing up surrounded by the apple trees, and how she had gone to art school in Scotland and ended up meeting her grandfather.

Adele paused in her story and they all changed the water in their buckets to rinse the areas they had just washed. For such a small space, it sure had a lot of nooks and crannies and shelves, Iris thought. There was also the deep glass-enclosed display case that her grandmother said would soon be filled with homemade brownies and cookies, scones and muffins.

"You know, Iris, Christmas in Scotland wasn't

really celebrated very widely until after World War II," she said, bringing a glossy shine to the old red counters with a thick white polish, "and it didn't even become a work holiday until the 1950's! There were actual laws against celebrating Christmas for hundreds of years."

"*Why*?" asked Iris, thinking that was the weirdest thing she had ever heard.

"The Protestants were not in favor of anything they viewed as Catholic. From what I have read, they believed it would take away from the reverence and solemn respect due to the Lord. Too much frivolity distracting from the true message. The people who believed this were the people in power, so that's just how it was for a very long time. The big celebration was Hogmanay and was celebrated at New Years. But I'm sure by now the Christmas season is celebrated every bit as cheerily there as it is here in the U.S."

As she scrubbed, she told Iris about the little Christmas fair in Inverness, and how she'd met her grandfather by selling him Christmas tree ornaments. As he was studying trees and working for the Forestry Commission, Christmas trees were a natural topic to discuss on their first date.

The decision to change the apple orchards to a Christmas tree farm was an easy one for them, even for her father, and made soon after they were married.

"The rest, as they say, is history," she said, drying off the shelf. "Let's just hope *we're* not history!"

After a very early breakfast the next morning,

Iris used the leftover fir, pine and cedar boughs hauled out of the barn to weave around the windows and doorways of the Emporium, the barn, and sheds. She thought she would never get the sticky pitch off her hands until her grandmother brought out a special dispenser from under the sink. Iris could tell her grandmother had painted the spruce boughs and cones on the glass container.

"This is our secret weapon, Iris," she said, squirting some kind of slippery, golden liquid into her cupped hands. It smelled a little like French fries, Iris thought, but with just a little scrubbing, the pitch began to dissolve.

Iris suspected that Howard had sent Daniel off to be a kind of Paul Revere, because, by the time the sun had fully risen, friends from around Placerville started to arrive, many in work clothes, many showing up with covered dishes to feed the crew, and even Father Kevin brought a large pot of what her grandmother called his famous turkey soup.

Others brought baked goods to sell in the Emporium. Gail Henderson, her Dad's old girlfriend she told Iris, but now married to Pete, the bus driver who dropped her off at the farm the night she arrived, had set up a table just off the parking lot where volunteers and customers could sign a petition to stop the eminent domain action.

"You should see it, Ashley!" she said, holding

her cell phone in one hand and hanging candy canes and icicle ornaments on the window trimmings with the other. "There are people everywhere!" While she decorated and talked with Ashley, she watched customers come and go, some pausing to visit with Adele and Charles, almost everyone carrying a cup of something hot and purchasing ornaments and treats, along with their trees.

"Tired?" Adele asked as Charles lay back against the pillows and groaned.

He didn't open his eyes as she slipped in beside him. "Aye," he answered with a weary smile, "but I'd rather be bone tired from work than weary from boredom any day. And thank you for not mollycoddling, even though I see you want to."

"You're welcome," she said, leaning over to kiss him, "as long as you promise to slow down when you need to. We've got plenty of help, bless everyone." She pulled the quilts over them and turned off the bedside lamp. "Speaking of helpers, Iris was asleep as soon as her head hit the pillow. I think she had just enough oomph left to climb into her pajamas and under the covers. Have you ever seen a child work as hard or be so eager to learn?"

"I expect she's trying to make up for lost time. She'll take home plenty of memories, that's for sure."

"And a first crush, too. She is absolutely smitten

with Daniel!"

"What?"

"You must have seen the way she looks at him!"

"The lass is only twelve!"

"A perfect age for a first love! And Daniel is so sweet—he'll never let on that he's noticed, or tease her in any way," she sighed. "Just more memories of her first visit."

"Let's just hope it's not her only visit," Charles said, opening his arms and she nestled in, her head on his shoulder.

The light of the waning moon shone through the lace at the window reminding Charles of another night when Adele had talked about Iris, although she had no memory of it.

"What does your *darna shealladh* tell you, *mo chridhe*?" he asked, his voice soft, "what is to become of us?"

"It was Granny MacIntyre that had the Sight, Charles."

Although she could not remember what happened that April night eleven years before, his own memory of the event could still spook him.

He had watched, appreciating how the moonlight had revealed her soft curves through her nightgown as she had stood before the open window, enjoying the warm spring breeze and glow of the full moon. He truthfully hadn't been paying attention to what she was saying —some harmless gossip she had heard in town, until she had suddenly stopped in the midst of her tale, becoming still. After several moments, in her own voice, but somehow softer, she had delivered what could only be called a prophecy. Remembering sent the gooseflesh springing up on his arms.

"You knew the lass would come, and that she would be alone when she did. Stood right there in front of me—still gives me the chills when I think of it."

"I'm not sure if I'm sad or grateful not to remember," she said, smoothing her warm hand over his forearm. "But it's true, even though I don't remember saying it, I've always been sure she would come; I just didn't know when or how. As for what will happen—I just can't see us anywhere else, Charles. Truly. Whether that's wishful thinking or the Sight," she paused, raising her head to kiss him again, "Weel, hinny, I canna be sure."

Chapter Twenty-Two

DEEP IN THE NIGHT, Iris woke suddenly from a sound sleep. The house was still and quiet until there was a creak on the floor just outside her room. She heard a soft knock on her door.

"Iris?" said an unfamiliar whisper.

"Yes?" she whispered back, heart hammering. She sat up as the door opened, the shaft of light from the hallway slowly widening.

"Don't be scared. I'm your uncle Alex."

He came in holding Darby, who was wagging his tail so hard Alexander could hardly keep hold of him. "Sorry to wake you up, kid, but I just got here and wanted to meet you before everyone was up."

"Hi! I didn't know you were coming," Iris said, turning on the light and fighting back a yawn.

"Nobody does, except Dan; he's the one who called me." Alexander sat down on the chair by the desk and put Darby down on the bed. "Mom wouldn't want to bother me about a little thing like this and Dad is probably still too mad at me to ask for my help. But I bet you've heard that already!"

"I saw your pictures in the photo albums," she said, rubbing her eyes.

"I've seen you, too!" he said, pausing and laughing at her expression. "Only when you were little, though! I bet, no, I *know* Mom and Dad were thrilled when you showed up out of the blue. Anyway, Dan picked me up in Sacramento a couple hours ago and we've been up all night. We're going to my room to crash— do me a favor? Tell your Grandma we're here and to save us some breakfast?"

When Iris told her grandmother that Alexander was upstairs in his room asleep, her eyes lit up and she was on her way up the stairs, but then she stopped and gave Iris a rueful smile before putting on her coat and going outside. Probably, thought Iris, just like the night she arrived, to prepare Charles with the news of an unexpected arrival.

By the time she came back inside, there were loud crashes and bangs from above.

"Alexander was eight years younger than Andrew and Daniel is six years younger than Alexander. They've been like brothers all these years, even though they are so different. Like Andrew, Daniel is so serious and Alexander is like a big, happy...puppy," Adele added, smiling, turning towards the stairs. "And that, my dear, is the sound of this house most of the time when the boys were growing up."

Footsteps were pounding down the stairs and Alexander burst into the living room, Daniel right behind him.

"Oh my dear, it's so wonderful to have you home!" his mother cried, catching him up in a hug. As soon as her arms were around him, she began to cry.

"Don't cry, Mom, geez," Alexander said, patting her back, which didn't help.

Iris looked at Daniel at the same time he looked at her, both wondering if they should leave the room, but by that time, Alexander had all the crying he could take.

"Dinna fash yersel, ye auld bletherskite! Palavering till yer peely-wally, and I hae to shoogle and skelp ye!" Alexander grimaced and played at wresting Adele's arms from around his neck while Darby barked and Daniel and Iris laughed at the stream of broad Scots. It was funny that even though she hadn't ever heard the words before, she knew just what they meant...sort of. Soon Adele was laughing, too, but that didn't stop Alexander.

"Be guan, into the kitchen wi' ye, woman! Parr-rrritch an' tatties, scones and shor--rrtbrrread on the double!" Iris was impressed with how well he rolled his r's. "Or me and Dan are going to McDonald's for Egg McMuffins!"

It was interesting, Iris thought later, but puppy was a

good description for Alexander. He seemed to bound from one thing to the next, one person to the other but always taking care of projects and making people happy along the way. Whenever he saw her he tickled her or teased her about her red hair, which was exactly the same as his own.

Just after the first rush of customers, a reporter from the local paper came to interview Charles and Adele. While they were taking a photograph of the family standing by the Family Tree sign, Iris was trying not to laugh because Alexander was tickling her just as the photographer was ready to snap the picture.

"Alexander, that's enough now!" scolded Adele.

"But Mom," he said, offended, "that's what uncles are supposed to do!"

The volume of customers increased. Many offered to help, some even insisted. Some purchased a second tree for a friend, others helped behind the counter to sell hot cocoa or cider. One lady threw her heavy fur coat over a step ladder, rolled up her sleeves and went to work stocking the display case with individually wrapped pieces of fudge that had just been delivered.

Even though Iris knew her grandparents were worried, it seemed to her that they were happy being open. Charles was stronger than ever, and even on his feet most of the day and walking without any help at all, either supervising the work or visiting with customers. Adele seemed to be able to talk with anyone about anything, always with a smile and remembering many customers by name. Several girls from town were drawn back to the farm once they knew that Alexander was home.

Charles, Adele, and Alexander kept Iris busy in turns, in the gift shop, the barn, or out in the field. Iris lost count of how many people she was introduced to over the week and whether they were old friends, returning customers, or someone they had never met before.

Amidst all the activity, though, a sad feeling began to creep in, especially when people talked about returning year after year. One old couple from Sacramento talked about how driving out and selecting a tree had been part of their holiday tradition for more than twenty years. Another was a newly married couple; the woman said she had come to The Family Tree to get a Christmas tree with her family as long as she could remember, and it was a tradition she insisted on keeping, even if her new husband had grown up with a "phony" tree.

This special place belonged to her family, but so many people had more memories of it and closer connections with it than she did. The feeling grew stronger the closer the time came for her to leave. Christmas Eve was on Friday and that meant one more day of sales, but only a few more hours for Iris since she was to leave on the bus south the next afternoon.

They closed that night in a somber mood. Alexander and Daniel had gone into town, and her grandparents rested while dinner was in the oven.

Iris went to her room and called home but no one answered, which was strange at dinnertime because they *never* took those boys out to a restaurant for dinner. She called Jennifer's cell.

"Hi Mom! Where are you?" Iris asked, hearing the twins screeching in the background even through the bad connection.

"Just some last-minute Christmas shopping, honey. How are you?"

"Not shopping! Driving, driving, driving," hollered one of the boys.

"You know those two, even going to the Mall is a long drive," Jennifer laughed, "How are you doing, honey? Are you worn out yet?"

"Tired, I guess, but not worn out. What's for dinner tomorrow?" she asked, now feeling both sad to be leaving her grandparents so soon and feeling homesick at the sound of her mother's laugh.

"All your favorites, kiddo. I better go before we lose the signal. Love you! See you tomorrow night at the bus station!"

Iris sat holding her phone. Now she was sad about leaving *and* feeling rejected.

Mom didn't miss her much at all, Iris thought. Jennifer would normally have all kinds of instructions before Iris did anything like riding a bus for hundreds of miles with total strangers, like, to call her every twenty minutes or something?

Chapter Twenty-Three

ADELE WAS ON THE PHONE when Iris came downstairs a few minutes later and Charles asked her to help him finish closing up the barn and sheds and turn off the lights for the night.

Heavy gray clouds had come in late in the afternoon, blocking out the sun and making it even colder

"What do you think, will start raining again, wee Gibson?"

Iris glanced up, surprised. She had been so happy earlier when that knowing feeling had come to her, she couldn't believe she'd forgotten to tell her mom. She had only seen snow a few times in her life.

"No! It's going to snow!"

Charles looked at her for a moment, then at the leaden sky and back to her.

"I think you may be right about that, lass. I hope so. At this temperature, rain is sure to make for icy roads and few customers..." he stopped as they saw a blue minivan, just like the one Eric had taken her for a test drive in just after Thanksgiving that he planned on surprising her mom with for Christmas.

The van pulled into the parking area that was still brightly lit with strands of Christmas lights. "I don't recognize the car, must be a late customer," Charles said.

"I'll go talk with them, Grandpa. If they're here for a tree, I'll ask them to come back tomorrow."

"If they're just after one that's cut, let them come and choose one, lass. We don't need an army to sell one Christmas tree."

When she reached the parking lot, two familiar little boys came running toward her, shaggy dark hair flopping in their eyes.

"Iris! Surprise! Surprise, Iris!" Harry and Heath screamed as they ran to her, hugging her legs and jumping up and down so hard that she could barely stand.

She looked up to see her mom and Eric walking towards her. Iris pulled the boys along with her as she went to meet them.

"Mom! What are you doing here?" she cried, hugging her and squishing one of the twins in the process.

"When your grandmother and I talked last time, she invited us to come for Christmas. I really missed you, sweetheart." Iris saw the tears in her eyes. "And I just couldn't stand the thought of you riding the bus with strangers again, especially at Christmas."

"And we wanted to help," added Eric, reaching

over to hug her, too. It was a big hug, not just tousling her hair like he usually did. "Can't let you have all the fun."

Iris hugged the boys so they would stop jumping on her as Eric and Jennifer shook hands with Charles.

"So, Mr. Gibson, I hear Iris has been as helpful here as she is at home," Eric said as they started towards the house.

With his eyes, Charles smiled at Iris, who was holding hands with the boys. "By now, the lass could probably run the place by herself. Come inside and meet Adele, she's been looking forward to meeting all of you."

Iris could see that her mom suddenly seemed nervous and whispered, "It's okay, Mom. Grandmother is really nice. You'll like her."

"You sound like me," Jennifer smiled, whispering back, "talking about your kindergarten teacher on your first day of school!"

Iris helped the boys build things with a new set of blocks that Adele had waiting in the closet. They didn't need any help, but it was a good place to sit and listen to the conversations between her grandfather and Eric and her mother and grandmother. It was hard to believe that just a few weeks ago her mom was so afraid of her meeting her grandparents and now they were all in the same room together.

When Adele excused herself to check on dinner, Iris took Jennifer over to the little alcove off the living room that was now open and illuminated.

"See this one, Mom?" she said, pointing out the one from the year she was born. "Remember I told you that in heraldry a fleur-de-lis is a symbol for an iris?"

"Look at that," said Jennifer, tracing over a golden fleur-de-lis with her finger. "It's beautiful. This place is beautiful and so are your grandparents, Iris."

Iris giggled, "I don't know what Grandpa would say about being called beautiful, Mom."

Jennifer laughed, too, "Okay, handsome, then."

She looked at Iris for a long while, almost, Iris thought, the way her grandmother did on that first night, almost like she was seeing Iris for the first time. "I want to apologize to you, honey, for not listening. I should have helped you find your grandparents. I was worried that Andrew's parents were like my mother and I was wrong."

Then she reached out and drew Iris into her arms and whispered into her ear, "But don't you dare even think about taking off to Seattle to look for your other grandmother, or you'll rue the day!"

Jennifer's tone of voice was light, but Iris remembered her father's last letter, how her grandmother had wanted her mother to have an abortion. She thought about the picture of her mom and dad together, their arms laced protectively over the baby Jennifer carried.

Just before they stepped out of the alcove, Darby

started barking and howling, the way he did only when he knew Alexander was near.

"Alexander and Daniel must be back," Iris said.

"Hmmm, your grandmother told me about Daniel. Cute, is he?"

"Mom!" Iris laughed, glancing back at her but Jennifer was now staring at Alexander. He and Daniel stood taking off their coats and petting the dog to get him to be still. The little boys, drawn to the commotion, had abandoned their blocks and were in the mix as well. Jennifer had paused in mid-step after seeing Alexander talking and laughing.

"He looks a little like my Dad, doesn't he?" asked Iris, giving her mother a worried look. "I guess I've gotten used to him...Grandma says he's like a big puppy."

Jennifer gave a small, shaky laugh. "Well, then, you better introduce us and we'll see if he knows how to shake hands!"

"Dad, I don't like this," It was Harry's usual dinnertime declaration, but at least this time he whispered. Eric glanced up to see if Adele had heard.

She just smiled. "You know, Eric, I started to make this dinner for my boys a long time ago because it was Spiderman's favorite dinner. Did you know that, young man?" She asked Heath, the shy one, who smiled and then hid behind Eric's shoulder.

"Yeah," said Iris to Eric. "I read in a magazine

that it's Iron Man's favorite, too!"

With that, Harry picked up his spoon and tried a bite.

Eric said to Iris, "And the Hulk's, too, isn't it?"

Heath put on his Hulk face and growled, "Smash!" picked up his fork and dug in with gusto.

"I'll need to remember that t- r -i -c- k, Mrs. Gibson," said Eric, amazed at the sight of the two boys now eating without a fuss.

"Adele," she reminded him to call her with a smile. "I have a bit of experience with a couple of fussy boys."

Alexander stopped eating and turned to Iris, stricken. "You mean it's *not* Spiderman's favorite?"

Iris listened to the conversations around the table; about the threat to the farm, the response from the community, and Charles and Adele praising Iris's work, from baking pies to harvesting trees. Iris noticed halfway through dinner how Eric made comments or asked questions that kept the conversation moving and comfortable.

After dinner, Alexander insisted on helping in the kitchen.

"Run along now, run along you two," he said, in a high, warbling Julia Child kind of voice, when Iris and Jennifer began to help. Trying to tie a frilly apron he'd unearthed from one of the kitchen drawers seemed to challenge him, though, so he turned his back to Daniel and held up the long ties. "Be a dahling, would you?"

From the amount of noise soon emanating from the kitchen, Iris thought Daniel must have tied Alexander to one of the kitchen chairs.

"You must think I'm the worst parent in the world, not being able to keep track of this one," Jennifer said, reaching out and stroking Iris's hair, as though reassuring herself they were together again.

The commotion in the kitchen had subsided to the subtler sounds of Daniel and Alexander washing dishes. The rest of them had settled into the living room.

"I think every parent loses track of their children at least once along the way," Adele said, "both Andrew and Alexander were independent spirits and wandered off a time or two. Believe me, my dear, I know just how you feel."

Her grandmother went on to recount a few episodes when each boy had taken to the road for one reason or another.

"Sheriff Abbot brought Andrew back after he decided to walk down to Placerville. He was nine. Alexander had just learned to walk and Andrew wanted to get away from his pesky little brother."

Jennifer smiled, but Iris saw she was really worried.

"I promise I won't do it again, Mom," she said.

"Well, there is still one grandparent you haven't met. You might strike out for Seattle one day soon."

"I *never* want to see her," Iris said, with such forcefulness that her mother's eyes widened in surprise.

Iris looked away and saw her grandfather watching them. He didn't smile, and there wasn't so much of a smile in his eyes as sympathy.

Eric joined them in the now very peaceful living room after the overtired twins fell asleep in the guest room. Even Alexander and Daniel were now talking quietly as they came into the living room and sat on the floor near Iris.

"I think we should tell them, Adele," Charles said.

"What's that?"

"Jennifer shouldna be blaming herself for what happened."

Iris watched her grandparents. Her grandfather was quite serious, and her grandmother had gone pale again, almost as pale as the night that Iris had arrived.

"An dà shealladh is the Gaelic for 'the second sight'," Adele began to explain after a long pause, "my great-grandmother, granny MacIntyre, was famous for it, she would often 'know' things before anyone else – the birth of a child, the failure of a crop or when we might expect a visitor, sometimes a death. My grandfather did not believe she shared everything she sensed, and she was apparently quite generous with her scoldings if anyone ever asked her to foretell their future, as though she were a gypsy!

"I occasionally have strong feelings, what you might think of as hunches or gut instincts that I am very aware of, but the few times I have truly 'seen', I have no memory of it," she paused and turned to Charles. "you should rightfully tell the story, as you were the only witness."

Iris felt the goosebumps prickle along her arms as her grandfather described the spring night in detail, the soft pine-scented breeze, the full moon and how her grandmother had stood at the open window of her bedroom. In a voice not quite her own, Charles continued, Adele had foretold Iris's arrival, and that she would come alone.

"Wow," Alexander said during the long silence that followed, making everyone laugh.

Everyone except Jennifer, who was looking at Alexander strangely.

"Have you ever been shocked?" She asked him. "severely?"

Iris saw a dismayed kind of surprise cross his face, but he recovered quickly.

"Shocked...? You mean like when Loki took over Asgard? Or when Jon Snow got done-in on Game of Thrones...?"

Jennifer wasn't distracted. "About six, no, seven years ago?"

"What is it, my dear?" Adele prompted.

"When Iris was..." Jennifer closed her eyes for a moment, then opened them again and continued, "five, in the middle of summer and it was a hot, hot night. She was restless, unusually agitated even with the heat, but finally fell asleep. The next thing I know, she's standing at the window of our room, talking to someone, but definitely not to me."

The room was silent again except for the instrumental Christmas music playing softly in the background.

Iris felt goosebumps again when her mom turned to her because Iris could tell she was still seeing the little Iris in her memory. "I couldn't make out the words, but you were most definitely carrying on a conversation. I got up and stood next to you, thinking you were talking and walking in your sleep.

"Then you looked up at me, wide awake, and said, 'There was a big flash and my uncle was dead.' 'was?' I asked, even then I was amazed I could keep my voice calm! And then you...you smiled..."

Tears filled her eyes and her voice faltered. She paused a moment before continuing, "...your father's smile...the biggest, happiest smile, and said 'Yep, but he's okay now!' And then you walked back to your bed, hopped in, grabbed your little bunny and went right back to sleep.

"I don't have a brother," Jennifer said, looking once again at Alexander, along with everyone else in the room.

Alex covered his face with his hands and fell backwards onto the floor.

"Iris, Iris, Iris," he muttered. "Ye bluidy wee

clipe."

"*What*?" She asked impatiently. "What happened to you?"

"You snitch! You tattle-tale, you … I thought I had gotten away with the biggest secret of my entire life! And then you, you, like a…like a…"

"Lightning bolt out of the blue?" Daniel supplied helpfully, with a smirk.

"Oh my God," Adele whispered, covering her own face with her hands. Charles put an arm around her shoulders and barked at Alexander, "Out with it!"

Resigned and now serious, Alexander sat up again.

"It was the summer I was sixteen when I spent a weekend with Jim and Ron in Yosemite. I know," he sort of bowed towards his mother, "you told me no, you told me I was too young, that you were worried something would happen, that you didn't know the guys well enough. But, I told you I was going to Sean's and went with them anyway.

"Even high up in the hills it was hot, and we didn't even notice the storm coming on until the air cooled a bit and the breeze came up, no warning rumbles of thunder or flashes of light in the distance.

"I had just gotten to sleep, only to be woken up by a couple of damn raccoons fighting over something near the creek where we were camped. Jim was still awake, sitting at the picnic table, calmly reading by lantern light, while Ron and I were throwing rocks at the raccoons—right at their beady little eyes that were glowing in the dark—when all of a sudden, the first flash blinded us and the thunder practically knocked us off our feet. My skin was tingling, I could smell ozone...and then I saw an odd blue glow and Ron's hair standing straight up. Jim yelled something, and I must have understood because I fell down to crouch on the balls of my feet just before the tree at the edge of the creek exploded."

Even Alexander couldn't make this story funny, Iris thought, reaching out and taking his hand. He glanced at her and smiled, but she could see that his mind was still on the vivid memory of that night.

"Thunder, when lightning hits that close, isn't just thunder, you're sure the earth has to open up and swallow you whole. That's the only thought I had before...well, before I passed out."

He looked at Charles and Adele for a long moment. "I remember it as a real memory, seeing Andrew. We were both so happy to see each other, I remember hugging him something fierce, but I can't remember feeling it, isn't that weird?" He asked Iris. She nodded, and she could tell her eyes were bugged out because he laughed at her and squeezed her hand. "I wanted to stay with him but he said no...actually he said, 'no way, butthead, you're goin' back' and I started to argue with him, but he said heid doon arse up wi' ye lad! ..." Alexander added with a grin but iris saw his smile disappear and followed his gaze. Her grandparents were pale, waiting for the rest of the story, almost as though Alexander was still in danger.

Being Alexander, he went on to regale them with the rest of his story, starting with his outraged sensibilities when he woke up to find Ron's mouth on his and Jim's hands on his chest, sitting up so fast he sent the two of them flying backwards.

"We ended up having the last laugh, though," Alexander said, lying back on the floor next to Iris again, "The next morning, when we found those damn raccoons?" He put all fours straight up in the air. "They were toast!"

Once laughter had eased the tension, the visitors, including Daniel, all said goodnight and went upstairs, leaving Alexander to the mercy of his parents.

"It'll be nice to see where you've been sleeping all these nights you've been away from home—"

At her sharp intake of breath, Iris saw that her mother's eyes were on her father's picture.

"I took that picture," she said, after a long while, sitting down on the bed, "and *that's* the smile I saw on your face that night. What a beautiful smile."

"What was so funny, Mom? What was he laughing at?" Iris asked, sitting next to her.

"At you!"

"Me?"

"I was looking at him through the camera lens when I told him I was pregnant, that you were on the way. That was the look on his face at that very moment. He was *so* happy about you." Jennifer's voice cracked, and Iris could see tears welling in her eyes again. "I know I already told you, but I am so sorry, Iris. I should have stayed in touch with your grandparents, but I was just so afraid of losing you."

She paused to take a tissue from the box on the nightstand. "My mom had come down after Andrew died. I think it was she who put me into an early labor. She wanted me to put you up for adoption because she was afraid that I would dump you on her—as if I would *ever* do that to you! My friends insisted that Andrew's parents were very nice, but when they had offered to take care of you, it just sounded like another way to take you away from me."

"When Grandmother and I talked the first night, she said that it might have been all you could do, taking care of me when you were so sad."

"I was sad." Jennifer wiped more tears from her face. "I think I was the saddest person in the world for a while." She sat quietly looking at the pictures for a few moments. "But you helped me through it, Iris. Every morning you would greet me with the biggest smile and the brightest eyes, and each night we would cuddle before you went to sleep. As you grew older you began to look more and more like Andrew…"

"I know you told me about him and showed me some pictures, but I really feel like I know him now, being here, reading his letters and seeing all of his pictures and stuff. Did you know that he wanted to move back here with us?"

Jennifer shook her head and Iris stood up and

got the letter from the desk drawer. Jennifer unfolded it carefully and her tears began to fall again when she saw the photograph. She closed her eyes for a moment and held it against her heart before reading the letter. When she finished, she folded the letter carefully and slipped it and the picture back into its envelope.

"Why didn't he tell you, Mom?"

"Probably because of how I felt about my mother. I *did* come home after that Christmas swearing I would never see her again. And I was happy being on our own and thought he was, too. Most of what I'd heard about his teenage years was early in our relationship when he talked about the constant work around here day after day. But I knew he felt differently once he came back after helping that Christmas, just like he said. He was probably waiting…," she reached out and stroked Iris's silky red hair, "…waiting for you."

They sat quietly for a few moments.

"Iris, are you sure your grandfather isn't taking the medication anymore?"

"Really sure. And now even Grandmother admits he's much better. Why? Did you find out anything?"

"I did, and I'll talk to them in the morning," Jennifer said, standing up. "Now, I had better get some sleep so I can keep up with you tomorrow. Give me a hug."

Chapter Twenty-Four

TWO INCHES OF DRY, fluffy snow blanketed everything when they woke the next morning. After another early breakfast, Eric went with Charles to unlock the barn and sheds while Daniel and Alexander went out to cut more trees to stock the barn.

The twins played quietly with their new Legos in front of the TV and Jennifer brought up the conversation that she and Iris had about Charles's medication.

"I work at a hospital overseeing insurance claims, so Iris knew that I could find out about the medication, Mrs. Gibson. I'm sorry to invade your privacy, but as you might have noticed, Iris can be very persuasive."

"Please call me Adele, my dear, and no apology necessary. We don't have any secrets."

"Is Charles ill with a thyroid condition?"

"Thyroid?" Adele asked, puzzled. "No, it's a heart condition. Why do you ask?"

"Well, Iris was worried when she heard her

grandfather say he thought the medication was making him worse instead of better."

When her grandmother looked at her, eyebrow raised, Iris wondered if she was about to get another helping of tongue pie. But as she told her grandmother about the television show with the exposé about improperly prescribed medication, Adele's expression softened immediately and she reached out and patted Iris's hand.

"From what Iris told me," Jennifer went on, "the prescription bottle says one thing, but the identifiers that she noted from the pills themselves show that it's a different medication, for people with a low functioning thyroid."

Adele stood up and retrieved the prescription bottle from a cabinet near the refrigerator. "The doctor said that Charles had a weak heart, and that was why he had such a time recovering from a bad bout of the flu last winter. He prescribed this for him last summer and never said anything about thyroid problems. He increased the dose about a month ago, and then again several days ago, but Charles refused to take any more of them."

"Why did he increase the dose?" Jennifer asked. "Did he explain?"

Adele didn't answer immediately, but turned away from them and gazed out the window. After a moment, she turned back to them, and her eyes met Jennifer's, and Iris could see something like fear in her expression.

"He said Charles was adjusting to the dose and it needed to be strengthened to keep helping…"

Jennifer lay down a napkin and spilled out the contents of the bottle onto the table and examined the bottle and pills carefully.

"The bottle clearly states that this should be Digoxin and yet the tablets are not. I printed this out for you to see what the pharmaceutical company imprints on each tablet," she said, unfolding the paper for Adele. "Did you pick this up at a pharmacy, or was it mailed to you?"

Adele shook her head. "Neither. The doctor always insists on bringing it himself. I can't understand how he could have made such a mistake."

"Adele, when he raised the dosage, were there any of the previous tablets left over?"

Iris saw their eyes meet again in understanding and Adele quickly left the table.

"Mom, will Grandpa be okay?"

"I'm sure he will, sweetheart."

Adele returned to the kitchen with a second medicine bottle. She opened it and tipped out one tablet onto the napkin. Jennifer read the name on the label and the markings on the pill. Adele put her glasses on as Jennifer moved the printout closer to her.

"This is the same thyroid medication, just a lower dose." She said it in almost a whisper and it seemed to Iris that her mother looked frightened now, too.

"Jennifer, what are the side-effects for someone

who doesn't need this medication?"

Jennifer pointed to a highlighted section on the printout. "The symptoms of the adverse effects may be similar to what someone with a heart condition might experience – easily fatigued, breathless, muscle weakness, heart palpitations, sometimes weight loss..."

"Dr. Alford was so insistent that we not open this year. He said the stress would be too much for Charles," she said, sinking down in her chair, her face drained of color.

"Mrs. Gibson! Adele, are you all right?"

"Dr. Alford?" Iris asked. She knew what her grandmother was thinking. "He owns the land right next to ours, right? And he's the dad of that woman that was here the other day, the one from the commission?"

"Oh my God," Adele said, covering her face with her hands, "it can't possibly be...?"

"Adele, there may be some other uses for this medication I'm not aware of, or possibly a mistake?"

"No, I don't think so, Jennifer," she answered, shaking her head. "Charles complained several times that he thought it made him feel worse, especially last month after the dose was changed. And I...how could I have been so foolish?"

"He's your doctor," Jennifer said, reaching out to put her hand on Adele's. "We're supposed to be able to trust our doctors. If you think there is some connection to this attempt to take your property, well then, you need to report this to the police."

Sherriff Abbot responded to Adele's call immediately and was at the farm even before Charles and Eric had returned to the house. He took the bottle of medication, as well as statements from Charles, Adele, and Jennifer and left promising to get to the bottom of things.

Eric, Jennifer, and Iris remained inside while Charles and Adele saw him to his car. Iris stood behind Jennifer and put her arms around her.

"Thank you, Mom," she whispered.

Eric leaned over and whispered in Iris's ear in a very bad Bogart imitation, "What d'ya say you and I go call on that doctor and beat the...living daylights out of him? Just you and me, kid?"

Even though she knew he was joking, his eyes weren't smiling now.

"I'd say that would be the beginning of a beautiful friendship."

Alexander and Daniel were already helping several early customers with trees when they all came outside. Clouds overhead were clearing to reveal a bright, blue sky. When she reached the barn, two trucks were just pulling in the driveway.

"Plumfield Farms" on one, in bright purple letters formed a semi-circle around a Christmas tree. The other truck, from "Gold Country Trees" had gold lettering with a glittering gold tree standing in for the T, and two workers were unloading balers and spools of netting from the truck bed.

A lady near the Plumfield truck turned and smiled at them as they approached.

"Morning, Charles."

"Good morning, Meg," her grandfather said, "Hello, Rich," he added, as the Gold Country driver ambled over. He shook hands with both. "This is my granddaughter, Iris. Iris, this is Meg Lawrence from Plumfield and Rich Lennox from Gold Country. Now then, not to be rude, folks, but what the hell is going on?"

Iris saw Meg and Rich exchange glances.

"Well, you see Charles," said Rich, "We're out of trees. Not a stick left."

Meg nodded. "So we thought we'd come on over and help you sell yours."

Wow, thought Iris, their farms must be really small if they ran out of trees. What were they going to sell next year?

Meg put her arm around Charles's shoulder to give him a one-armed hug. He seemed unable to respond. "You wouldn't want us to be bored and left out of the end of season fun, would you?"

Charles shook his head, and his voice sounded even gruffer than usual, "It's too much. I canna ask it of either of you—"

"You're not asking, you stubborn old Scot," Rich laughed.

"And neither are we," Meg added. "Don't think of it as charity, Charles. It's not charity – it's a fight! You know you'd do exactly the same thing if it were one of us in trouble. Now, tell us where to set up, and we'll try to stay out of your way."

Charles went with them and Iris walked over to where one of the Plumfield workers was unloading.

"Are you really out of trees?" Iris asked.

The girl laughed. "No, we've still got plenty, but that didn't stop Mom from closing up. Once she heard about what was happening, she got on the phone and talked Rich into this invasion. Where's a plug for this, do you know?"

Iris showed her an outlet on the side of the shed.

"And we're not just closed, either," said a man, unloading the final spool of net from the Gold Country truck. "There are signs up on both places, directing customers here. Business will boom today!"

Boom it did, with a steady stream of customers throughout the morning, a few regular customers from all three farms, but most were newcomers brought by the newspaper article that had appeared in newspapers and on Facebook newsfeeds everywhere.

Gail Henderson had to add a second notebook for signatures for the petition.

Late in the afternoon, just before the final closing of the season, Iris saw a long white van drive up the driveway. Antennas and a satellite dish were on top and San Francisco NEWS was written along the side in big, blue letters. It didn't stop at the parking lot, but continued to wend its way slowly past all the cars, people, trees and equipment to park near the house. Mr. Lennox walked over to the van.

"Hey, Dad!" said a pretty woman with spiky blond hair.

"Hey yourself, kiddo!" he said, giving her a big hug. "How's everything?"

"Everything's perfect, but we've got about five minutes before we go live! Where's our star"

Star? Iris thought, glancing around as they walked towards her.

"Lacy Lennox, meet Iris Gibson. Iris, this is my daughter and, as you've probably guessed by now, she's a reporter."

"Hey, Iris! It's great to meet you," Lacy said, reaching out to shake her hand "Your dad and I were good buddies growing up."

"Nice to meet you, too. Who's the star?" Iris looked around to see if she could see anyone she recognized.

Lacy laughed. "Tell you what, honey, come over here and watch and let's see if you recognize her when you see her." She steered Iris over to where Jade, one of the cameramen was setting up outside the Emporium. "You'll just have to wait a few more minutes, okay?"

Iris nodded, excited at the thought of meeting someone famous, but feeling guilty for sitting down on the job when she should be working. Lacy did say it would only be another few minutes, though, and she watched as Lacy talked with Miles, the other cameraman, who nodded and smiled at something she was telling him. After walking over to Charles and Adele and talking with them for a few minutes, Lacy went to stand in front of the barn where Miles was aiming the camera. Iris watched Jade video the workers from all three Christmas tree farms helping bale trees and haul them to the parking lot. Then she noticed that Miles was aiming a camera at her!

Another car was driving in, a really fancy one and Iris wondered if the star was inside but couldn't see beyond the tinted windows. Only a man she didn't recognize got out and stood beside it, watching Lacy and the cameramen do their work.

He looked as fancy and out of place as his car did, dressed in a dark gray suit and a blue tie that was just about the color of the sky overhead. Iris saw Howard walk up and shake hands with him. When Lacy started to speak, the men turned their attention to her and so did Iris.

"This is Lacy Lennox reporting to you from just outside my hometown of Placerville, at The Family Tree Christmas tree farm owned by Charles and Adele Gibson.

"I'm proud to declare a bit of bias on this story, folks, because I grew up on a neighboring tree farm and these people are like family to me.

"Two days before Christmas, a Christmas tree farm is a wonderful place to work and visit, and the activity that you see around me is what you might expect from a thriving Christmas tree farm during its busy season..."

Iris watched as Jade moved the camera lens towards the window of the Emporium, where Fran could be seen helping customers from behind the counter and a couple of little kids were sitting on the steps drinking cocoa. Miles moved his camera towards the barn, catching Daniel lifting a tree onto his shoulder and following a family out to their car. He smiled and winked at Iris as he passed by.

Iris felt something... something like one of those big, pink pompom fireworks she had seen last New Year's, explode in the top part of her stomach. Her face got hot and it was suddenly hard to breathe. *Wow*, she thought, wait till Ashley hears about *that*! She watched him walk away, trying to fix that wink, that *smile*, in her memory and almost didn't hear what Lacy Lennox had to say next.

"...but, except for the intervention of one little angel at the top, *this* Family Tree might not have lived to see next season. I am pleased to tell you about a new local hero, a young lady who almost single-handedly brought down a multi-layered, high-financed plot to grasp this treasured local business from her family."

Iris looked around to see who they were talking about and saw that most of the activity had stopped. The man in the blue tie had a pained expression on his face, but Charles and Adele, Jennifer and Eric were now standing to one side smiling at her. Alexander and

Daniel, and all of the customers and volunteers were standing by, smiling at her too. When she turned back to watch Lacy, Iris saw Jade's camera aimed right at her. Before she could react, Miles's camera was on Lacy and she was talking again. Talking about her! How she had found her family through a school assignment, how she had brought the warning of the eminent domain action initiated by a few villains in their local government, and how she may have uncovered a plot to keep her family from opening this season.

The man in the suit walked up to Lacy and she introduced him as Gavin Rycroft, president of the Sierra Recreation Group.

"Mr. Rycroft, I know you have just learned about these events from Sheriff Abbott, and as there is an ongoing investigation, we won't go into details here. But I know you would like to say a few words to the family and to our viewers."

Iris noticed that Mr. Rycroft seemed a little nervous himself when the camera was on him and she felt nervous about what he was going to say.

"First, Lacy, thank you for giving me this opportunity to assure everyone here and in your viewing audience that the Sierra Recreation Group was not aware of and in no way condones the tactics employed by the few individuals involved to acquire the Gibson property.

"The Sierra Recreation Group's mission has always been to promote healthy lifestyles, fitness, and recreation. I deeply regret the stress and injury that might have been imposed on this family and this community. We are suspending our plan to develop the area near the High Creek Reservoir—"

A cheer rippled through the crowd and Mr. Rycoft stopped looking so grim and smiled before continuing, "We will review all possible options, and any further discussion involving local access will involve the *entire* community!"

Amid the cheering, Lacy Lennox signed off with a dramatic promise of a full exposé. Iris felt hands on her shoulders and looked up to see her grandfather standing behind her.

"*Guardian* angel at the top of the tree is more like it, wee Gibson," he said, leaning down and whispering something else in Gaelic, words which didn't need any translation.

The day after Christmas, Iris was sitting in her very own seat in the back of the new van, thinking about all that had happened since she rode the bus north just over a week before. Everything had been so uncertain. What were her grandparents like, what did the farm look like, and most of all, what was her place in their family?

Now, transplanting the uncertainty were memories of planting trees, baking pies, decorating windows, and her mother and grandmother shedding tears as they hugged goodbye.

Alexander was the hardest one to say goodbye to and he was so serious when he hugged her. Iris remembered the story about the night he had been hit by lightning, when they had both, somehow, seen her father. Knowing they shared that, even if she couldn't remember, gave her that happy-sad feeling again.

The semester was over and it was too late to use all the photographs, newspaper clippings and enough family information on her father's side to fill a Giant Sequoia, but the grade she received didn't really matter.

She had something even better, she thought, reaching into her backpack for the red silk box and removing the ornament her grandmother had painted just for her.

A beautifully decorated evergreen, and perched precariously on top, a smiling, red-headed angel.

Acknowledgements

&

Author Information

 *Original artwork by* **K**endall **R**oss

To my sister Becky, for assigning *Devil Water* by Anya Seton as an 8th-grade homeschool English & History assignment — an ominous title, but with very positive ripples. To my sister Debi, not generally a reader of fiction, who gave one of the best (?) compliments after reading an early draft of *The Family Tree* – "...it was so good, I kept having to remind myself that *you* wrote it!" To my sister Sharrie, who shared the book with her friends, which resulted in a very nice Fran letter. And, to my mother, Babe, who loved the book and promoted it to pretty much anyone who would listen.

My thanks to Lella Mack, dear friend and steadfast writing partner of eight years, for her thorough and honest critiques, and more recently, for the excellent feedback and support from members of the Fairbanks Community Writers Group.

A special dedication to the late novelist Anya Seton, in appreciation of her gift for bringing history so vibrantly to life, and for responding to each and every letter a certain 15-year-old fan ever wrote with kindness, patience, and always the encouragement to write.

Cynthia Rinear Bethune was born and raised in
Fairbanks, Alaska. She has been a freelance feature
writer, ghostwriter, and is currently working on
her next two novels, *Brendan's Cross* and *You
Belong to Me*.

Visit on Facebook at
https://fb.me/authorCynthiaRinear

Made in the USA
Middletown, DE
04 January 2021

30353572R00137